Escape from the Shark's Belly

"We must find a way to escape," said Pinocchio.

"Escape?" said Gepetto. "But how?"

"We will escape through the mouth of the shark, into the sea, and then swim away!"

"That's all very well, dear Pinocchio—but I can't swim."

"I am a good swimmer. You can hang onto my back, and I'll carry you safely to the shore."

"It's no use, my boy," said Gepetto, with a sad smile, shaking his head. "A puppet like you, only three feet long, could not be strong enough to swim if I were on his back."

"Try it and you'll see!"

PINOCCHIO

Carlo Collodi

A TOM DOHERTY ASSOCIATES BOOK
NEW YORK

PINOCCHIO

A Tor Book
Published by Tom Doherty Associates, Inc.
175 Fifth Avenue
New York, NY 10010

Tor® is a registered trademark of Tom Doherty Associates, Inc.

ISBN: 0-812-56702-1

First Tor edition: May 1996

Printed in the United States of America

0 9 8 7 6 5 4 3 2 1

Contents

PINOCCHIO

Carlo Collodi

Carlo Collodi is the pen name of Carlo Lorenzini, a famous Italian writer of humble origins who was born in northern Italy in 1826. He took the name Collodi from his mother's birthplace in Tuscany. He went to school in Florence, where one assumes he met and befriended many of those upon whom he later based the characters in *Pinocchio*. After school, he trained for the priesthood and eventually became a journalist, founding his own newspaper and theatrical journal. In 1860 he became a government official with a specialized interest in education, and all his experiences culminated at this time in writing stories for children.

The Adventures of Pinocchio, originally titled "The Tale of a Puppet," was written as a serial for an illustrated children's weekly. It appeared in book form in 1883 and quickly sold a million copies in Italy alone. When the book became available in English in 1892, two years after Lorenzini's death, it was greeted with tremendous enthusiasm. It has been translated into over ninety languages, and has been a worldwide favorite ever since.

Foreword

Originally written as a serial, the thirty-six chapters in *Pinocchio* are each an individual adventure in the life of a good-hearted but misguided puppet.

Author Carlo Collodi is able to take liberties with a character carved from wood that he perhaps would not in a story about a real boy and his father. But a story about a well-intentioned, if easily influenced, puppet leaves us far enough removed from the action to be able to laugh at Pinocchio's antics, yet sympathize with his all-too-real feelings. The author invokes universal truths, making it easy for us to identify our own failings in Pinocchio's actions.

Far from being the story popularized in animated film and illustrated books for young children, the original *Pinocchio*, as translated from the Italian, opens with a carpenter about to make a table leg from a piece of ordinary wood. When he approaches the wood with an axe, the wood cries out to him.

Geppetto, a destitute puppet maker, calls on the carpenter about this time, seeking a piece of wood from which to carve a new puppet. Fueled by wisecracks from the innocuous-looking piece of wood, the two end up in a terrible fight. The carpenter gives the haunted piece of wood to Geppetto, who takes it home and begins to carve the puppet he fancies will make him rich and famous. It is the strangest carving experience he's ever had.

Pinocchio comes to life with too much spunk and too little common sense, which leads him into mischief and one disastrous adventure after another. Beginning with the first of his life's wrong turns, Pinocchio disregards Geppetto's instructions and goes to a puppet show instead of going to school. That detour leads to a seemingly endless set of wrong choices. He endeavors ever after to get back to his father, but every time the opportunity nears, Pinocchio sabotages his chance.

With just enough magic and absurdity to hold the attentions of the very young, the right amount of humor and adventure for young adults, and a lesson or two in morality for adults, *Pinocchio* is a story for all ages, for all seasons, for all time.

PINOCCHIO

Chapter I

How it came to pass that MASTER CHERRY *the carpenter found a piece of wood that laughed and cried like a child*

There was once upon a time ...

"A king!" my little readers will instantly exclaim.

No, children you are wrong. There was once upon a time a piece of wood.

This wood was not valuable: it was only a common log like those that are burnt in winter in the stoves and fireplaces to make a cheerful blaze and warm the rooms.

I cannot say how it came about, but the fact is that one fine day this piece of wood was lying in the shop of an old carpenter of the name of Master Antonio. He was, however, called by everybody Master Cherry, on account of the end of his nose, which was always as red and polished as a ripe cherry.

No sooner had Master Cherry set eyes on the piece of wood than his face beamed with delight; and, rubbing his hands together with satisfaction, he said softly to himself:

"This wood has come to the right moment; it will just do to make the leg of a little table."

Having said this he immediately took a sharp ax with

which to remove the bark and the rough surface. Just, however, as he was going to give the first stroke, he remained with his arm suspended in the air, for he heard a very small voice saying imploringly, "Do not strike me so hard!"

Picture to yourselves the astonishment of good old Master Cherry!

He turned his terrified eyes all round the room to try and discover where the little voice could possibly have come from, but he saw nobody! He looked under the bench—nobody; he looked into a cupboard that was always shut—nobody; he looked into a basket of shavings and sawdust—nobody; he even opened the door of the shop and gave a glance into the street—and still nobody. Who, then, could it be?

"I see how it is," he said, laughing and scratching his wig. "Evidently that little voice was all my imagination. Let us set to work again."

And taking up the ax he struck a tremendous blow on the piece of wood.

"Oh! Oh! You have hurt me!" cried the same little voice dolefully.

This time Master Cherry was petrified. His eyes started out of his head with fright, his mouth remained open, and his tongue hung out almost to the end of his chin, like a mask on a fountain. As soon as he had recovered the use of his speech, he began to say, stuttering and trembling with fear:

"But where on earth can that little voice have come from that said Oh! Oh!? Here there is certainly no living soul. Is it possible that this piece of wood can have learnt to cry and to lament like a child? I cannot believe it. This piece of wood, here it is; a log for fuel like all the others, and thrown on the fire it would about suffice to boil a saucepan of beans. . . . How then? Can anyone be hidden inside it? If anyone is hidden inside, so much the worse for him. I will settle him at once."

So saying, he seized the poor piece of wood and commenced beating it without mercy against the walls of the room.

Then he stopped to listen if he could hear any little voice lamenting. He waited two minutes—nothing; five minutes—nothing; ten minutes—still nothing!

"I see how it is," he then said, forcing himself to laugh and pushing up his wig. "Evidently the little voice that said Oh! Oh! was all my imagination! Let us set to work again."

Nevertheless, he was very frightened, so he tried to sing to give himself a little courage.

Putting the ax aside he took his plane, to plane and polish the bit of wood; but while he was running it up and down he heard the same little voice say laughing:

"Have done! You are tickling me all over!"

This time poor Master Cherry fell down as if he had been struck by lightning. When he at last opened his eyes he found himself seated on the floor.

His face was quite changed, even the end of his nose, instead of being crimson, as it was nearly always, had become blue from fright.

Chapter II

MASTER CHERRY *makes a present of the piece of wood to his friend* GEPPETTO, *who takes it to make for himself a wonderful puppet, that shall know how to dance, and to fence, and to leap like an acrobat*

At that moment someone knocked at the door.

"Come in," said the carpenter, without having the strength to rise to his feet.

A lively little old man immediately walked into the shop. His name was Geppetto, but when the boys of the neighborhood wished to put him in a passion they called him by the nickname of Polendina, because his yellow wig greatly resembled a pudding made of Indian corn.

Geppetto was very fiery. Woe to him who called him Polendina! He became furious, and there was no holding him.

"Good day, Master Antonio," said Geppetto. "What are you doing there on the floor?"

"I am teaching the alphabet to the ants."

"Much good may that do you."

"What has brought you to me, neighbor Geppetto?"

"My legs. But to say the truth, Master Antonio, I am come to ask a favor of you."

"Here I am, ready to serve you," replied the carpenter, getting on to his knees.

"This morning an idea came into my head."

"Let us hear it."

"I thought I would make a beautiful wooden puppet; but a wonderful puppet that should know how to dance, to fence, and to leap like an acrobat. With this puppet I would travel about the world to earn a piece of bread and a glass of wine. What do you think of it?"

"Bravo, Polendina!" exclaimed the same little voice, and it was impossible to say where it came from.

Hearing himself called Polendina, Geppetto became as red as a turkey cock from rage, and turning to the carpenter he said in a fury:

"Why do you insult me?"

"Who insults you?"

"You called me Polendina!"

"It was not I!"

"Would you have it, then, that it was I? It was you, I say!"

"No!"

"Yes!"

"No!"

"Yes!"

And becoming more and more angry, from words they came to blows, and flying at each other they bit, and fought, and scratched manfully.

When the fight was over, Master Antonio was in possession of Geppetto's yellow wig, and Geppetto discovered that the gray wig belonging to the carpenter had remained between his teeth.

"Give me back my wig," screamed Master Antonio.

"And you, return me mine, and let us make friends."

The two old men having each recovered his own wig shook hands, and swore that they would remain friends to the end of their lives.

"Well, then, neighbor Geppetto," said the carpenter, to prove that peace was made, "what is the favor that you wish of me?"

"I want a little wood to make my puppet; will you give me some?"

Master Antonio was delighted and he immediately went to the bench and fetched the piece of wood that had caused him so much fear. But just as he was going to give it to his friend the piece of wood gave a shake, and wriggling violently out of his hands struck with all of its force against the dried-up shins of poor Geppetto.

"Ah! Is that the courteous way in which you make your presents, Master Antonio? You have almost lamed me!"

"I swear to you that it was not I!"

"Then you would have it that it was I?"

"The wood is entirely to blame!"

"I know that it was the wood; but it was you that hit my legs with it!"

"I did not hit you with it!"

"Liar!"

"Geppetto, don't insult me or I will call you Polendina!"

"Ass!"

"Polendina!"

"Donkey!"

"Polendina!"

"Baboon!"

"Polendina!"

On hearing himself called Polendina for the third time Geppetto, blind with rage, fell upon the carpenter and they fought desperately.

When the battle was over, Master Antonio had two more scratches on his nose, and his adversary had two buttons too little on his waistcoat. Their accounts being thus squared, they shook hands and swore to remain good friends for the rest of their lives.

Geppetto carried off his fine piece of wood and, thanking Master Antonio, returned limping to his house.

Chapter III

GEPPETTO *having returned home begins at once to make a puppet, to which he gives the name of* PINOCCHIO. *The first tricks played by the puppet.*

Geppetto lived in a small ground-floor room that was only lighted from the staircase. The furniture could not have been simpler—a bad chair, a poor bed, and a broken-down table. At the end of the room there was a fireplace with a lighted fire; but the fire was painted, and by the fire was a painted saucepan that was boiling cheerfully, and sending out a cloud of smoke that looked exactly like real smoke.

As soon as he reached home Geppetto took his tools and set to work to cut out and model his puppet.

"What name shall I give him?" he said to himself. "I think I will call him Pinocchio. It is a name that will bring him luck. I once knew a whole family so called. There was Pinocchio the father, Pinocchia the mother, and Pinocchi the children, and all of them did well. The richest of them was a beggar."

Having found a name for his puppet he began to work

in good earnest, and he first made his hair, then his forehead, and then his eyes.

The eyes being finished, imagine his astonishment when he perceived that they moved and looked fixedly at him.

Geppetto, seeing himself stared at by those two wooden eyes, took it almost in bad part, and said in an angry voice:

"Wicked wooden eyes, why do you look at me?"

No one answered.

He then proceeded to carve the nose; but no sooner had he made it than it began to grow. And it grew, and grew, and grew, until in a few minutes it had become an immense nose that seemed as if it would never end.

Poor Geppetto tired himself out with cutting it off; but the more he cut and shortened it, the longer did that impertinent nose become!

The mouth was not even completed when it began to laugh and deride him.

"Stop laughing!" said Geppetto, provoked; but he might as well have spoken to the wall.

"Stop laughing, I say!" he roared in a threatening tone.

The mouth then ceased laughing, but put out its tongue as far as it would go.

Geppetto, not to spoil his handiwork, pretended not to see, and continued his labors. After the mouth he fashioned the chin, then the throat, then the shoulders, the stomach, the arms and the hands.

The hands were scarcely finished when Geppetto felt his wig snatched from his head. He turned round, and what did he see? He saw his yellow wig in the puppet's hand.

"Pinocchio! Give me back my wig instantly!"

But Pinocchio, instead of returning it, put it on his own head, and was in consequence nearly smothered.

Geppetto at this insolent and derisive behavior felt sadder and more melancholy than he had ever been in his life before; and turning to Pinocchio he said to him:

"You young rascal! You are not yet completed, and you are already beginning to show want of respect to your father! That is bad, my boy, very bad!"

And he dried a tear.

The legs and the feet remained to be done.

When Geppetto had finished the feet he received a kick on the point of his nose.

"I deserve it!" he said to himself. "I should have thought of it sooner! Now it is too late!"

He then took the puppet under the arms and placed him on the floor to teach him to walk.

Pinocchio's legs were stiff and he could not move, but Geppetto led him by the hand and showed him how to put one foot before the other.

When his legs became flexible Pinocchio began to walk by himself and to run about the room; until, having gone out of the house door, he jumped into the street and escaped.

Poor Geppetto rushed after him but was not able to overtake him, for that rascal Pinocchio leapt in front of him like a hare, and knocking his wooden feet together against the pavement made as much clatter as twenty pairs of peasants' clogs.

"Stop him! Stop him!" shouted Geppetto; but the people in the street, seeing a wooden puppet running like a race horse, stood still in astonishment to look at it, and laughed, and laughed, and laughed, until it beats description.

At last, as good luck would have it, a carabineer arrived who, hearing the uproar, imagined that a colt had escaped from his master. Planting himself courageously with his legs apart in the middle of the road, he waited with the determined purpose of stopping him, and thus preventing the chance of worse disasters.

When Pinocchio, still at some distance, saw the carabineer barricading the whole street, he endeavored to take him by surprise and to pass between his legs. But he failed sadly.

The carabineer without disturbing himself in the least caught him cleverly by the nose—it was an immense nose of ridiculous proportions that seemed made on purpose to be laid hold of by carabineers—and consigned him to Geppetto. Wishing to punish him, Geppetto intended to pull his ears at once. But imagine his feelings when he could not succeed in finding them. And do you know the reason? It was that, in his hurry to model him, he had forgotten to make them.

He then took him by the collar, and as he was leading him away he said to him, shaking his head threateningly:

"We will go home at once, and as soon as we arrive we will regulate our accounts, never doubt it."

At this announcement Pinocchio threw himself on the ground and would not take another step. In the meanwhile a crowd of idlers and inquisitive people began to assemble and to make a ring around them.

Some of them said one thing, some another.

"Poor puppet," said several, "he is right not to wish to return home! Who knows how Geppetto, that bad old man, will beat him!"

And the others added maliciously:

"Geppetto seems a good man, but with boys he is a regular tyrant! If that poor puppet is left in his hands he is quite capable of tearing him in pieces!"

It ended in so much being said and done that the carabineer at last set Pinocchio at liberty and conducted Geppetto to prison. The poor man, not being ready with words to defend himself, cried like a calf, and as he was being led away to prison sobbed out:

"Wretched boy! And to think how I have labored to make him a well-conducted puppet! But it serves me right! I should have thought of it sooner!"

What happened afterward is a story that really is past all belief, but I will relate it to you in the following chapters.

Chapter IV

The story of PINOCCHIO *and the* TALKING
CRICKET, *from which we see that naughty boys
cannot endure to be corrected by those who
know more than they do*

Well, then, children, I must tell you that while poor
Geppetto was being taken to prison for no fault of
his, that imp Pinocchio, finding himself free from the
clutches of the carabineer, ran off as fast as his legs could
carry him. That he might reach home the quicker he
rushed across the fields, and in his mad hurry he jumped
high banks, thorn hedges, and ditches full of water, exactly
as a kid or a leveret would have done if pursued by hunt-
ers.

Having arrived at the house he found the street door
ajar. He pushed it open, went in, and having secured the
latch, threw himself on the ground and gave a great sigh
of satisfaction.

But his satisfaction did not last long, for he heard someone in the room who was saying:

"Cri-cri-cri!"

"Who calls me?" said Pinocchio in a fright.

"It is I!"

Pinocchio turned round and saw a big cricket crawling slowly up the wall.

"Tell me, Cricket, who may you be?"

"I am the Talking Cricket, and I have lived in this room a hundred years and more."

"Now, however, this room is mine," said the puppet, "and if you would do me a pleasure go away at once, without even turning round."

"I will not go," answered the Cricket, "until I have told you a great truth."

"Tell it me, then, and be quick about it."

"Woe to those boys who rebel against their parents, and run away capriciously from home. They will never come to any good in the world, and sooner or later they will repent bitterly."

"Sing away, Cricket, as you please, and as long as you please. For me, I have made up my mind to run away tomorrow at daybreak, because if I remain I shall not escape the fate of all other boys. I shall be sent to school and shall be made to study either by love or by force. To tell you in confidence, I have no wish to learn; it is much more amusing to run after butterflies, or to climb trees and to take the young birds out of their nests."

"Poor little goose! But do you not know that in that way you will grow up a perfect donkey, and that everyone will make game of you?"

"Hold your tongue, you wicked ill-omened croaker!" shouted Pinocchio.

But the cricket, who was patient and philosophical, instead of becoming angry at this impertinence, continued in the same tone:

"But if you do not wish to go to school, why not at least learn a trade, if only to enable you to earn honestly a piece of bread!"

"Do you want me to tell you?" replied Pinocchio, who was beginning to lose patience. "Among all the trades in the world there is only one that really takes my fancy."

"And that trade—what is it?"

"It is to eat, drink, sleep, and amuse myself, and to lead a vagabond life from morning to night."

"As a rule," said the Talking Cricket with the same composure, "all those who follow that trade end almost always either in a hospital or in prison."

"Take care, you wicked ill-omened croaker! Woe to you if I fly into a passion!"

"Poor Pinocchio! I really pity you!"

"Why do you pity me?"

"Because you are a puppet and, what is worse, because you have a wooden head."

At these last words Pinocchio jumped up in a rage, and snatching a wooden hammer from the bench he threw it at the Talking Cricket.

Perhaps he never meant to hit him; but unfortunately it struck him exactly on the head, so that the poor Cricket had scarcely breath to cry Cri-cri-cri, and then he remained dried up and flattened against the wall.

Chapter V

PINOCCHIO *is hungry and searches for an egg to make himself an omelet; but just at the most interesting moment the omelet flies out of the window*

Night was coming on, and Pinocchio, remembering that he had eaten nothing all day, began to feel a gnawing in his stomach that very much resembled appetite.

But appetite with boys travels quickly, and in fact after a few minutes his appetite had become hunger, and in no time his hunger became ravenous—a hunger that was really quite insupportable.

Poor Pinocchio ran quickly to the fireplace where a saucepan was boiling, and was going to take off the lid to see what was in it, but the saucepan was only painted on the wall. You can imagine his feelings. His nose, which was already long, became longer by at least three fingers.

He then began to run about the room, searching in the drawers and in every imaginable place, in hope of finding a bit of bread. If it was only a bit of dry bread, a crust, a bone left by a dog, a little moldy pudding of Indian corn, a fishbone, a cherry stone—in fact anything that he could gnaw. But he could find nothing, nothing at all, absolutely nothing.

And in the meanwhile his hunger grew and grew; and poor Pinocchio had no other relief than yawning, and his yawns were so tremendous that sometimes his mouth almost reached the place where his ears should have been. And after he had yawned he spluttered, and felt as if he were going to faint.

Then he began to cry desperately, and he said:

"The Talking Cricket was right. I did wrong to rebel against my papa and to run away from home. If my papa were here I should not now be dying of hunger! Oh, what a dreadful illness hunger is!"

Just then he thought he saw something in the dust heap—something round and white that looked like a hen's egg. To give a spring and seize hold of it was the affair of a moment. It was indeed an egg.

Pinocchio's joy beats description; it can only be imagined. Almost believing it must be a dream, he kept turning the egg over in his hands, feeling it and kissing it. And as he kissed it he said:

"And now, how shall I cook it? Shall I make an omelet? . . . No, it would be better to cook it in a saucer! . . . Or would it not be more savory to fry it in the frying pan? Or shall I simply boil it? No, the quickest way of all is to cook it in a saucer: I am in such a hurry to eat it!"

Without loss of time he placed an earthenware saucer on a brazier full of red-hot embers. Into the saucer instead of oil or butter he poured a little water; and when the water began to smoke, tac! he broke the eggshell over it that the contents might drop in. But instead of the white and the yolk, a little chicken popped out very gay and polite. Making a beautiful curtsy it said to him:

"A thousand thanks, Master Pinocchio, for saving me the trouble of breaking the shell. Adieu until we meet again. Keep well, and my best compliments to all at home!"

Thus saying, it spread its wings, darted through the open window, and flying away was lost to sight.

The poor puppet stood as if he had been bewitched,

with his eyes fixed, his mouth open, and the eggshell in his hand. Recovering, however, from his first stupefaction, he began to cry and scream, and to stamp his feet on the floor in desperation, and amidst his sobs, he said:

"Ah, indeed the Talking Cricket was right. If I had not run away from home, and if my papa were here, I should not now be dying of hunger! Oh, what a dreadful illness hunger is!"

And as his stomach cried out more than ever and he did not know how to quiet it, he thought he would leave the house and make an excursion in the neighborhood in hope of finding some charitable person who would give him a piece of bread.

Chapter VI

PINOCCHIO *falls asleep with his feet on the brazier, and wakes in the morning to find them burnt off*

It was a wild and stormy winter's night. The thunder was tremendous and the lightning so vivid that the sky seemed on fire. A bitter blusterous wind whistled angrily, and raising clouds of dust swept over the country, causing the trees to creak and groan as it passed.

Pinocchio had a great fear of thunder, but hunger was stronger than fear. He therefore closed the house door and made a rush for the village, which he reached in a hundred bounds, with his tongue hanging out and panting for breath, like a dog after game.

But he found it all dark and deserted. The shops were closed, the windows shut, and there was not so much as a dog in the street. It seemed the land of the dead.

Pinocchio, urged by desperation and hunger, laid hold of the bell of a house and began to peal it with all his might, saying to himself:

"That will bring somebody."

And so it did. A little old man appeared at a window with a nightcap on his head, and called to him angrily:

"What do you want at such an hour?"

"Would you be kind enough to give me a little bread?"

"Wait there, I will be back directly," said the little old man, thinking he had to do with one of those rascally boys who amuse themselves at night by ringing the house bells to rouse respectable people who are sleeping quietly.

After half a minute the window was again opened, and the voice of the same little old man shouted to Pinocchio:

"Come underneath and hold out your cap."

Pinocchio had no cap; but as he stood under the window, an enormous basin of water was poured down on him, watering him from head to foot as if he had been a pot of dried-up geraniums.

He returned home like a wet chicken quite exhausted with fatigue and hunger; and having no longer strength to stand, he sat down and rested his damp muddy feet on a brazier full of burning embers.

And then he fell asleep; and while he slept, his feet, which were wooden, took fire, and little by little they burnt away and became cinders.

Pinocchio continued to sleep and to snore as if his feet belonged to someone else. At last about daybreak he awoke because someone was knocking at the door.

"Who is there?" he asked, yawning and rubbing his eyes.

"It is I!" answered a voice.

And the voice was Geppetto's voice.

Chapter VII

Poor Pinocchio, whose eyes were still half shut from sleep, had not as yet discovered that his feet were burnt off. The moment, therefore, that he heard his father's voice he slipped off his stool to run and open the door; but after stumbling two or three times he fell his whole length on the floor.

And the noise he made in falling was as if a sack of wooden ladles had been thrown from a fifth story.

"Open the door!" shouted Geppetto from the street.

"Dear Papa, I cannot," answered the puppet, crying and rolling about on the ground.

"Why cannot you?"

"Because my feet have been eaten."

"And who has eaten your feet?"

"The cat," said Pinocchio, seeing the cat, who was amusing herself by making some shavings dance with her forepaws.

"Open the door, I tell you!" repeated Geppetto. "If you

don't, when I get into the house you shall have the cat from me!"

"I cannot stand up, believe me. Oh, poor me, poor me! I shall have to walk on my knees for the rest of my life!"

Geppetto, believing that all this lamentation was only another of the puppet's tricks, thought of a means of putting an end to it, and climbing up the wall he got in at the window.

He was very angry, and at first he did nothing but scold; but when he saw his Pinocchio lying on the ground and really without feet he was quite overcome. He took him in his arms and began to kiss and caress him and to say a thousand endearing things to him, and as the big tears ran down his cheeks, he said, sobbing:

"My little Pinocchio! How did you manage to burn your feet?"

"I don't know, Papa, but believe me it has been an infernal night that I shall remember as long as I live. It thundered and lightened, and I was very hungry, and then the Talking Cricket said to me: 'It serves you right; you have been wicked and you deserve it,' and I said to him: 'Take care, Cricket!' . . . and he said: 'You are a puppet and you have a wooden head,' and I threw the handle of a hammer at him, and he died, but the fault was his, for I didn't wish to kill him, and the proof of it is that I put an earthenware saucer on a brazier of burning embers, but a chicken flew out and said: 'Adieu until we meet again, and many compliments to all at home': and I got still more hungry, for which reason that little old man in a nightcap opening the window said to me, 'Come underneath and hold out your hat,' and poured a basinful of water on my head, because asking for a little bread isn't a disgrace, is it? And I returned home at once, and because I was always very hungry I put my feet on the brazier to dry them, and then you returned, and I found they were burnt off, and I am always hungry, but I have no longer any feet! Ih! Ih! Ih! Ih! . . ." And poor Pinocchio began to cry and to roar so loudly that he was heard five miles off.

Geppetto, who from all this jumbled account had only understood one thing, which was that the puppet was dying of hunger, drew from his pocket three pears, and giving them to him said:

"These three pears were intended for my breakfast; but I will give them to you willingly. Eat them, and I hope they will do you good."

"If you wish me to eat them, be kind enough to peel them for me."

"Peel them?" said Geppetto, astonished. "I should never have thought, my boy, that you were so dainty and fastidious. That is bad! In this world we should accustom ourselves from childhood to like and to eat everything, for there is no saying to what we may be brought. There are so many chances! . . ."

"You are no doubt right," interrupted Pinocchio, "but I will never eat fruit that has not been peeled. I cannot bear rind."

So that good Geppetto fetched a knife, and arming himself with patience peeled the three pears, and put the rind on a corner of the table.

Having eaten the first pear in two mouthfuls, Pinocchio was about to throw away the core; but Geppetto caught hold of his arm and said to him:

"Do not throw it away; in this world everything may be of use."

"But core I am determined I will not eat," shouted the puppet, turning upon him like a viper.

"Who knows! There are so many chances! . . ." repeated Geppetto without losing his temper.

And so the three cores, instead of being thrown out of the window, were placed on the corner of the table together with the three rinds.

Having eaten, or rather having devoured the three pears, Pinocchio yawned tremendously, and then said in a fretful tone:

"I am as hungry as ever!"

"But, my boy, I have nothing more to give you!"

"Nothing, really nothing?"

"I have only the rind and the cores of the three pears."

"One must have patience!" said Pinocchio. "If there is nothing else I will eat a rind."

And he began to chew it. At first he made a wry face; but then one after another he quickly disposed of the rinds; and after the rinds even the cores, and when he had eaten up everything he clapped his hands on his sides in his satisfaction, and said joyfully:

"Ah! Now I feel comfortable."

"You see now," observed Geppetto, "that I was right when I said to you that it did not do to accustom ourselves to be too particular or too dainty in our tastes. We can never know, my dear boy, what may happen to us. There are so many chances! . . ."

Chapter VIII

GEPPETTO *makes* PINOCCHIO *new feet, and sells his own coat to buy him a spelling book*

No sooner had the puppet appeased his hunger than he began to cry and to grumble because he wanted a pair of new feet.

But Geppetto, to punish him for his naughtiness, allowed him to cry and to despair for half the day. He then said to him:

"Why should I make you new feet? To enable you, perhaps, to escape again from home?"

"I promise you," said the puppet, sobbing, "that for the future I will be good."

"All boys," replied Geppetto, "when they are bent upon obtaining something, say the same thing."

"I promise you that I will go to school, and that I will study and earn a good character."

"All boys, when they are bent on obtaining something, repeat the same story."

"But I am not like other boys! I am better than all of them and I always speak the truth. I promise you, Papa, that I will learn a trade, and that I will be the consolation and the staff of your old age."

Geppetto, although he put on a severe face, had his eyes full of tears and his heart big with sorrow at seeing his poor Pinocchio in such a pitiable state. He did not say another word, but taking his tools and two small pieces of well-seasoned wood he set to work with great diligence.

In less than an hour the feet were finished: two little feet—swift, well-knit, and nervous. They might have been modeled by an artist of genius.

Geppetto then said to the puppet:

"Shut you eyes and go to sleep!"

And Pinocchio shut his eyes and pretended to be asleep.

And while he pretended to sleep, Geppetto, with a little glue which he had melted in an eggshell, fastened his feet in their place, and it was so well done that not even a trace could be seen of where they were joined.

No sooner had the puppet discovered that he had feet than he jumped down from the table on which he was lying, and began to spring and to cut a thousand capers about the room, as if he had gone mad with the greatness of his delight.

"To reward you for what you have done for me," said Pinocchio to his father, "I will go to school at once."

"Good boy."

"But to go to school I shall want some clothes."

Geppetto, who was poor, and who had not so much as a farthing in his pocket, then made him a little jacket of flowered paper, a pair of shoes from the bark of a tree, and a cap of a crumb of bread.

Pinocchio ran immediately to look at himself in a crock of water, and he was so pleased with his appearance that he said, strutting about like a peacock:

"I look quite like a gentleman!"

"Yes, indeed," answered Geppetto, "for bear in mind that it is not fine clothes that make the gentleman, but rather clean clothes."

"By the bye," added the puppet, "to go to school I am

still in want—indeed I am without the best thing, and the most important."

"And what is it?"

"I have no spelling book."

"You are right; but what shall we do to get one?"

"It is quite easy. We have only to go to the bookseller's and buy it."

"And the money?"

"I have got none."

"No more have I," added the good old man very sadly.

And Pinocchio, although he was a very merry boy, became sad also; because poverty, when it is real poverty, is understood by everybody—even by boys.

"Well, patience!" exclaimed Geppetto, all at once rising to his feet, and putting on his old fustian coat, all patched and darned, he ran out of the house.

He returned shortly, holding in his hand a spelling book for Pinocchio, but the old coat was gone. The poor man was in his shirt sleeves, and out of doors it was snowing.

"And the coat, Papa?"

"I have sold it."

"Why did you sell it?"

"Because I found it too hot."

Pinocchio understood this answer in an instant, and unable to restrain the impulse of his good heart he sprang up, and throwing his arms around Geppetto's neck he began kissing him again and again.

Chapter IX

A s soon as it had done snowing Pinocchio set out for school with his fine spelling book under his arm. As he went along he began to imagine a thousand things in his little brain, and to build a thousand castles in the air, one more beautiful than the other.

And talking to himself he said:

"Today at school I will learn to read at once; then tomorrow I will begin to write, and the day after tomorrow to cipher. Then with my acquirements I will earn a great deal of money, and with the first money I have in my pocket I will immediately buy for my papa a beautiful new cloth coat. But what am I saying? Cloth, indeed! It shall be all made of gold and silver, and it shall have diamond buttons. That poor man really deserves it; for to buy my book and have me taught he has remained in his shirt sleeves. . . . And in this cold! It is only fathers who are capable of such sacrifices! . . ."

While he was saying this with great emotion he thought that he heard music in the distance that sounded like fifes and the beating of a big drum: fi-fi-fi, fi-fi-fi, zum, zum, zum, zum.

He stopped and listened. The sounds came from the end of a cross street which led to a little village on the sea-shore.

"What can that music be? What a pity that I have to go to school, or else . . ."

And he remained irresolute. It was, however, necessary to come to a decision. Should he go to school? Or should he go after the fifes?

"Today I will go and hear the fifes, and tomorrow I will go to school," finally decided the young scape-grace, shrugging his shoulders.

The more he ran the nearer came the sounds of the fifes and the beating of the big drum: fi-fi-fi, zum, zum, zum, zum.

At last he found himself in the middle of a square quite full of people, who were all crowding round a building made of wood and canvas, and painted a thousand colors.

"What is that building?" asked Pinocchio, turning to a little boy who belonged to the place.

"Read the placard—it is all written—and then you will know."

"I would read it willingly, but it so happens that today I don't know how to read."

"Bravo, blockhead! Then I will read it to you. The writing on that placard in those letters red as fire is:

'GREAT PUPPET THEATER.' "

"Has the play begun long?"

"It is beginning now."

"How much does it cost to go in?"

"Twopence."

Pinocchio, who was in a fever of curiosity, lost all control of himself, and without any shame he said to the little boy to whom he was talking:

"Would you lend me twopence until tomorrow?"

"I would lend them to you willingly," said the other, taking him off, "but it so happens that today I cannot give them to you."

"I will sell you my jacket for twopence," the puppet then said to him.

"What do you think that I could do with a jacket of flowered paper? If there was rain and it got wet, it would be impossible to get it off my back."

"Will you buy my shoes?"

"They would only be of use to light the fire."

"How much will you give me for my cap?"

"That would be a wonderful acquisition indeed! A cap of bread crumb! There would be a risk of the mice coming to eat it while it was on my head."

Pinocchio was on thorns. He was on the point of making another offer, but he had not the courage. He hesitated, felt irresolute and remorseful. At last he said:

"Will you give me twopence for this new spelling book?"

"I am a boy and I don't buy from boys," replied his little interlocutor, who had much more sense than he had.

"I will buy the spelling book for twopence," called out a hawker of old clothes, who had been listening to the conversation.

And the book was sold there and then. And to think that poor Geppetto had remained at home trembling with cold in his shirt sleeves, that he might buy his son a spelling book.

Chapter X

The puppets recognize their brother PINOCCHIO, *and receive him with delight; but at that moment their master,* FIRE-EATER, *makes his appearance and* PINOCCHIO *is in danger of coming to a bad end*

When Pinocchio came into the little puppet theater, an incident occurred that almost produced a revolution. I must tell you that the curtain was drawn up, and the play had already begun.

On the stage Harlequin and Punchinello were as usual quarreling with each other, and threatening every moment to come to blows.

The audience, all attention, laughed till they were ill as they listened to the bickering of these two puppets, who gesticulated and abused each other so naturally that they might have been two reasonable beings, and two persons of the world.

All at once Harlequin stopped short, and turning to the public he pointed with his hand to someone far down in the pit, and exclaimed in a dramatic tone:

"Gods of the firmament! Do I dream, or am I awake? But surely that is Pinocchio!"

"It is indeed Pinocchio!" cried Punchinello.

"It is indeed himself!" screamed Miss Rose, peeping from behind the scenes.

"It is Pinocchio! It is Pinocchio!" shouted all the puppets in chorus, leaping from all sides on to the stage. "It is Pinocchio! It is our brother Pinocchio! Long live Pinocchio!"

"Pinocchio, come up here to me," cried Harlequin, "and throw yourself into the arms of your wooden brothers!"

At this affectionate invitation Pinocchio made a leap from the end of the pit into the reserved seats; another leap landed him on the head of the leader of the orchestra, and he then sprang upon the stage.

The embraces, the hugs, the friendly pinches, and the demonstrations of warm brotherly affection that Pinocchio received from the excited crowd of actors and actresses of the puppet dramatic company beat description.

The sight was doubtless a moving one, but the public in the pit, finding that the play was stopped, became impatient and began to shout: "We will have the play—go on with the play!"

It was all breath thrown away. The puppets, instead of continuing the recital, redoubled their noise and outcries, and putting Pinocchio on their shoulders they carried him in triumph before the footlights.

At that moment out came the showman. He was very big, and so ugly that the sight of him was enough to frighten anyone. His beard was as black as ink, and so long that it reached from his chin to the ground. I need only say that he trod upon it when he walked. His mouth was as big as an oven, and his eyes were like two lanterns of red glass with lights burning inside them. He carried a large whip made of snakes' and foxes' tails twisted together, which he cracked constantly.

At his unexpected appearance there was a profound silence: no one dared to breathe. A fly might have been heard in the stillness. The poor puppets of both sexes trembled like so many leaves.

"Why have you come to raise a disturbance in my the-

ater?" asked the showman of Pinocchio, in the gruff voice
of a hobgoblin suffering from a severe cold in the head.

"Believe me, honored sir, that it was not my fault! . . ."

"That is enough! Tonight we will settle our accounts."

As soon as the play was over the showman went into
the kitchen where a fine sheep, preparing for his supper,
was turning slowly on the spit in front of the fire. As there
was not enough wood to finish roasting and browning it,
he called Harlequin and Punchinello, and said to them:

"Bring that puppet here: you will find him hanging on
a nail. It seems to me that he is made of very dry wood,
and I am sure that if he were thrown on the fire he would
make a beautiful blaze for the roast."

At first Harlequin and Punchinello hesitated; but, ap-
palled by a severe glance from their master, they obeyed.
In a short time they returned to the kitchen carrying poor
Pinocchio, who was wriggling like an eel taken out of water, and screaming desperately:

"Papa, Papa, save me! I will not die, I will not die! . . ."

Chapter XI

FIRE-EATER sneezes and pardons PINOCCHIO, *who then saves the life of his friend* HARLEQUIN

The showman Fire-eater—for that was his name—looked, I must say, a terrible man, especially with the black beard that covered his chest and legs like an apron. On the whole, however, he had not a bad heart. In proof of this, when he saw poor Pinocchio brought before him, struggling and screaming, "I will not die, I will not die!" he was quite moved and felt very sorry for him. He tried to hold out, but after a little he could stand it no longer and he sneezed violently. When he heard the sneeze, Harlequin, who up to that moment had been in the deepest affliction, and bowed down like a weeping willow, became quite cheerful, and leaning toward Pinocchio he whispered to him softly:

"Good news, brother. The showman has sneezed, and that is a sign that he pities you, and consequently you are saved."

For you must know that while most men, when they feel compassion for somebody, either weep or at least pretend to dry their eyes, Fire-eater, on the contrary, whenever he was really overcome, had the habit of sneezing.

After he had sneezed, the showman, still acting the ruffian, shouted to Pinocchio:

"Have done crying! Your lamentations have given me a pain in my stomach.... I feel a spasm, that almost ... Etci! Etci!" and he sneezed again twice.

"Bless you!" said Pinocchio.

"Thank you! And your papa and your mamma, are they still alive?" asked Fire-eater.

"Papa, yes; my mamma I have never known."

"Who can say what a sorrow it would be for your poor old father if I were to have you thrown among those burning coals! Poor old man! I compassionate him! ... Etci! Etci! Etci!" and he sneezed again three times.

"Bless you!" said Pinocchio.

"Thank you! All the same, some compassion is due to me, for as you see I have no more wood with which to finish roasting my mutton, and to tell you the truth, under the circumstances you would have been of great use to me! However, I have had pity on you, so I must have patience. Instead of you I will burn under the spit one of the puppets belonging to my company. Ho there, gendarmes!"

At this call two wooden gendarmes immediately appeared. They were very long and very thin, and had on cocked hats, and held unsheathed swords in their hands.

The showman said to them in a hoarse voice:

"Take Harlequin, bind him securely, and then throw him on the fire to burn. I am determined that my mutton shall be well roasted."

Only imagine that poor Harlequin! His terror was so great that his legs bent under him and he fell with his face on the ground.

At this agonizing sight Pinocchio, weeping bitterly, threw himself at the showman's feet, and bathing his long beard with his tears he began to say in a supplicating voice:

"Have pity, Sir Fire-eater! ..."

"Here there are no sirs," the showman answered severely.

"Have pity, Sir Knight! . . ."

"Here there are no knights!"

"Have pity, Commander! . . ."

"Here there are no commanders!"

"Have pity, Excellence! . . ."

Upon hearing himself called Excellence the showman began to smile, and became at once kinder and more tractable. Turning to Pinocchio, he asked:

"Well, what do you want from me?"

"I implore you to pardon poor Harlequin."

"For him there can be no pardon. As I have spared you, he must be put on the fire, for I am determined that my mutton shall be well roasted."

"In that case," cried Pinocchio proudly, rising and throwing away his cap of bread crumb—"in that case I know my duty. Come on, gendarmes! Bind me and throw me among the flames. No, it is not just that poor Harlequin, my true friend, should die for me!"

These words, pronounced in a loud heroic voice, make all the puppets who were present cry. Even the gendarmes, although they were made of wood, wept like two newly born lambs.

Fire-eater at first remained as hard and unmoved as ice, but little by little he began to melt and to sneeze. And having sneezed four or five times, the showman opened his arms affectionately and said to Pinocchio:

"You are a good, brave boy! Come here and give me a kiss."

Pinocchio ran at once, and climbing like a squirrel up the showman's beard he deposited a hearty kiss on the point of his nose.

"Then the pardon is granted?" asked poor Harlequin in a faint voice that was scarcely audible.

"The pardon is granted!" answered Fire-eater; he then added, sighing and shaking his head:

"I must have patience! Tonight I shall have to resign

myself to eat the mutton half raw; but another time woe to him who chances! ..."

At the news of the pardon the puppets all ran to the stage, and having lighted the lamps and chandeliers as if for a full-dress performance, they began to leap and to dance merrily. At dawn they were still dancing.

Chapter XII

The showman, FIRE-EATER, *makes* PINOCCHIO *a present of five gold pieces to take home to his father,* GEPPETTO, *but* PINOCCHIO *instead allows himself to be taken in by the* FOX *and the* CAT, *and goes with them*

The following day Fire-eater called Pinocchio on one side and asked him:

"What is your father's name?"

"Geppetto."

"And what trade does he follow?"

"He is a beggar."

"Does he gain much?"

"Gain much? Why, he has never a penny in his pocket. Only think, to buy a spelling book for me to go to school he was obliged to sell the only coat he had to wear—a coat that, between patches and darns, was not fit to be seen."

"Poor devil! I feel almost sorry for him! Here are five gold pieces. Go at once and take them to him with my compliments."

You can easily understand that Pinocchio thanked the showman a thousand times. He embraced all the puppets of the company one by one, even to the gendarmes, and beside himself with delight set out to return home.

But he had not gone far when he met on the road a Fox lame of one foot and a Cat blind in both eyes, who were going along helping each other like good companions in misfortune. The Fox, who was lame, walked leaning on the Cat, and the Cat, who was blind, was guided by the Fox.

"Good day, Pinocchio," said the Fox, accosting him politely.

"How do you come to know my name?" asked the puppet.

"I know your father well."

"Where did you see him?"

"I saw him yesterday at the door of his house."

"And what was he doing?"

"He was in his shirt sleeves and shivering with cold."

"Poor Papa! But that is over; for the future he shall shiver no more!"

"Why?"

"Because I have become a gentleman."

"A gentleman—you!" said the Fox, and he began to laugh rudely and scornfully. The Cat also began to laugh, but to conceal it she combed her whiskers with her fore-paws.

"There is little to laugh at," cried Pinocchio angrily. "I am really sorry to make your mouth water, but if you know anything about it, you can see that these here are five gold pieces."

And he pulled out the money that Fire-eater had made him a present of.

At the sympathetic ring of the money the Fox, with an involuntary movement, stretched out the paw that seemed crippled, and the Cat opened wide two eyes that looked like two green lanterns. It is true that she shut them again, and so quickly that Pinocchio observed nothing.

"And now," asked the Fox, "what are you going to do with all that money?"

"First of all," answered the puppet, "I intend to buy a new coat for my papa, made of gold and silver, and with diamond buttons; and then I will buy a spelling book for myself."

"For yourself?"

"Yes, indeed: for I wish to go to school to study in earnest."

"Look at me!" said the Fox. "Through my foolish passion for study I have lost a leg."

"Look at me!" said the Cat. "Through my foolish passion for study I have lost the sight of both my eyes."

At that moment a white Blackbird, that was perched on the hedge by the road, began his usual song, and said:

"Pinocchio, don't listen to the advice of bad companions: if you do you will repent it!"

Poor Blackbird! If only he had not spoken! The Cat, with a great leap, sprang upon him, and without even giving him time to say Oh! ate him in a mouthful, feathers and all.

Having eaten him and cleaned her mouth she shut her eyes again and feigned blindness as before.

"Poor Blackbird!" said Pinocchio to the Cat. "Why did you treat him so badly?"

"I did it to give him a lesson. He will learn another time not to meddle in other people's conversation."

They had gone almost halfway when the Fox, halting suddenly, said to the puppet:

"Would you like to double your money?"

"In what way?"

"Would you like to make out of your five miserable sovereigns, a hundred, a thousand, two thousand?"

"I should think so! But in what way?"

"The way is easy enough. Instead of returning home you must go with us."

"And where do you wish to take me?"

"To the Land of the Owls."

Pinocchio reflected a moment, and then he said resolutely:

"No, I will not go. I am already close to the house, and I will return home to my papa who is waiting for me. Who can tell how often the poor old man must have sighed yesterday when I did not come back! I have indeed been a bad son, and the Talking Cricket was right when he said: 'Disobedient boys never come to any good in the world.' I have found it to my cost, for many misfortunes have happened to me. Even yesterday in Fire-eater's house I ran the risk ... Oh, it makes me shudder only to think of it!"

"Well, then," said the Fox, "you are quite decided to go home? Go then, and so much the worse for you."

"So much the worse for you!" repeated the Cat.

"Think well of it, Pinocchio, for you are giving a kick to fortune."

"To fortune!" repeated the Cat.

"Between today and tomorrow your five sovereigns would have become two thousand."

"Two thousand!" repeated the Cat.

"But how is it possible that they could have become so many?" asked Pinocchio, remaining with his mouth open from astonishment.

"I will explain it to you at once," said the Fox. "You must know that in the Land of the Owls there is a sacred field called by everybody the Field of Miracles. In this field you must dig a little hole, and you put into it, we will say, one gold sovereign. You then cover up the hole with a little earth: you must water it with two pails of water from the fountain, then sprinkle it with two pinches of salt, and when night comes you can go quietly to bed. In the meanwhile, during the night, the gold piece will grow and flower, and in the morning when you get up and return to the field, what do you find? You fine a beautiful tree laden with as many gold sovereigns as a fine ear of corn has grains in the month of June."

"So that," said Pinocchio, more and more bewildered, "supposing I buried my five sovereigns in that field, how many should I find there the following morning?"

"That is an exceedingly easy calculation," replied the Fox, "a calculation that you can make on the ends of your fingers. Put that every sovereign gives you an increase of five hundred: multiply five hundred by five, and the following morning you will find you with two thousand five hundred shining gold pieces in your pocket."

"Oh, how delightful!" cried Pinocchio, dancing for joy. "As soon as ever I have obtained those sovereigns, I will keep two thousand for myself, and the other five hundred I will make a present of to you two."

"A present to us?" cried the Fox with indignation and appearing much offended. "What are you dreaming of?"

"What are you dreaming of?" repeated the Cat.

"We do not work," said the Fox, "for dirty interest: we work solely to enrich others."

"Others!" repeated the Cat.

"What good people!" thought Pinocchio to himself; and forgetting there and then his papa, the new coat, the spelling book, and all his good resolutions, he said to the Fox and the Cat:

"Let us be off at once. I will go with you."

Chapter XIII

The inn of the RED CRAWFISH

They walked, and walked, and walked, until at last, toward evening, they arrived dead tired at the inn of the Red Crawfish.

"Let us stop here a little," said the Fox, "that we may have something to eat and rest ourselves for an hour or two. We will start again at midnight, so as to arrive at the Field of Miracles by dawn tomorrow morning."

Having gone into the inn they all three sat down to table: but none of them had any appetite.

The Cat, who was suffering from indigestion and feeling seriously indisposed, could only eat thirty-five mullet with tomato sauce, and four portions of tripe with Parmesan cheese; and because she thought the tripe was not seasoned enough, she asked three times for the butter and grated cheese!

The Fox would also willingly have picked a little, but as his doctor had ordered him a strict diet, he was forced to content himself simply with a hare dressed with a sweet and sour sauce, and garnished lightly with fat chickens and

early pullets. After the hare he sent for a dish made of par-
tridges, rabbits, frogs, lizards, and other delicacies; he
could not touch anything else. He had such a disgust to
food, he said, that he could put nothing to his lips.

The one who ate the least was Pinocchio. He asked for
some walnuts and a hunch of bread, and left everything on
his plate. The poor boy, whose thoughts were continually
fixed on the Field of Miracles, had got in anticipation an
indigestion of gold pieces.

When they had supped, the Fox said to the host:

"Give us two good rooms, one for Mr. Pinocchio, and
the other for me and my companion. We will snatch a little
sleep before we leave. Remember, however, that at midnight we wish to be called to continue our journey."

"Yes, gentlemen," answered the host, and he winked at
the Fox and the Cat, as much as to say: "I know what you
are up to. We understand one another!"

No sooner had Pinocchio got into bed than he fell asleep
at once and began to dream. And he dreamt that he was in
the middle of a field, and the field was full of shrubs covered with clusters of gold sovereigns, and as they swung
in the wind they went zin, zin, zin, almost as if they
would say: "Let who will, come and take us." But when
Pinocchio was at the most interesting moment, that is, just
as he was stretching out his hand to pick handfuls of those
beautiful gold pieces and to put them in his pocket, he was
suddenly awakened by three violent blows on the door of
his room.

It was the host who had come to tell him that midnight
had struck.

"Are my companions ready?" asked the puppet.

"Ready! Why, they left two hours ago."

"Why were they in such a hurry?"

"Because the Cat had received a message to say that her
eldest kitten was ill with chilblains on his feet, and was in
danger of death."

"Did they pay for the supper?"

"What are you thinking of? They are much too well ed-

ucated to dream of offering such an insult to a gentleman
like you."

"What a pity! It is an insult that would have given me
so much pleasure!" said Pinocchio, scratching his head. He
then asked:

"And where did my good friends say they would wait
for me?"

"At the Field of Miracles, tomorrow morning at daybreak."

Pinocchio paid a sovereign for his supper and that of his
companions, and then left.

Outside the inn it was so pitch dark that he had almost
to grope his way, for it was impossible to see a hand's
breadth in front of him. In the adjacent country not a leaf
moved. Only some night birds flying across the road from
one hedge to the other brushed Pinocchio's nose with their
wings as they passed, which caused him so much terror
that, springing back, he shouted, "Who goes there?" and
the echo in the surrounding hills repeated in the distance:
"Who goes there? Who goes there? Who goes there?"

As he was walking along he saw a little insect shining
dimly on the trunk of a tree, like a night light in a lamp
of transparent china.

"Who are you?" asked Pinocchio.

"I am the ghost of the Talking Cricket," answered the
insect in a low voice, so weak and faint that it seemed to
come from the other world.

"What do you want with me?" said the puppet.

"I want to give you some advice. Go back, and take the
four sovereigns that you have left to your poor father, who
is weeping and in despair because you have not returned
to him."

"By tomorrow my papa will be a gentleman, for these
four sovereigns will have become two thousand."

"Don't trust, my boy, those who promise to make you
rich in a day. Usually they are either mad or rogues! Give
ear to me, and go back."

"On the contrary, I am determined to go on."

"The hour is late!"

"I am determined to go on."

"The night is dark!"

"I am determined to go on."

"The road is dangerous!"

"I am determined to go on."

"Remember that boys who are bent on following their caprices, and will have their own way, sooner or later repent it."

"Always the same stories. Good night, Cricket."

"Good night, Pinocchio, and may Heaven preserve you from dangers and from assassins."

No sooner had he said these words than the Talking Cricket vanished suddenly like a light that has been blown out, and the road became darker than ever.

Chapter XIV

PINOCCHIO, *because he would not heed the good counsels of the* TALKING CRICKET, *falls among assassins*

Really," said the puppet to himself as he resumed his journey, "how unfortunate we poor boys are. Everybody scolds us, everybody admonishes us, everybody gives us good advice. To let them talk, they would all take it into their heads to be our fathers and our masters—all: even the Talking Cricket. See now; because I don't choose to listen to that tiresome cricket, who knows, according to him, how many misfortunes are to happen to me! I am even to meet with assassins! That is, however, of little consequence, for I don't believe in assassins—I have never believed in them. For me, I think that assassins have been invented purposely by papas to frighten boys who want to go out at night. Besides, supposing I was to come across them here in the road, do you imagine they would frighten me? Not the least in the world. I should go to meet them and cry: 'Gentlemen assassins, what do you want with me? Remember that with me there is no joking. Therefore go about your business and be quiet!' At this speech, said in a determined tone, those poor assassins—I think I see them—would run away like the wind. If, however, they were so badly educated as not to run away, why, then, I would run away myself, and there would be an end of it."

But Pinocchio had not time to finish his reasoning, for at that moment he thought that he heard a slight rustle of leaves behind him.

He turned to look, and saw in the gloom two evil-looking black figures completely enveloped in charcoal sacks. They were running after him on tiptoe, and making great leaps like two phantoms.

"Here they are in reality!" he said to himself, and not knowing where to hide his gold pieces he put them in his mouth precisely under his tongue.

Then he tried to escape. But he had not gone a step when he felt himself seized by the arm, and heard two horrid sepulchral voices saying to him:

"Your money or your life!"

Pinocchio, not being able to answer in words, owing to the money that was in his mouth, made a thousand low bows and a thousand pantomimes. He tried thus to make the two muffled figures, whose eyes were only visible through the holes in their sacks, understand that he was a poor puppet, and that he had not as much as a false farthing in his pocket.

"Come now! Less nonsense and out with the money!" cried the two brigands threateningly.

And the puppet made a gesture with his hands to signify "I have got none."

"Deliver up your money or you are dead," said the taller of the brigands.

"Dead!" repeated the other.

"And after we have killed you, we will also kill your father."

"Also your father!"

"No, no, no, not my poor papa!" cried Pinocchio in a despairing tone; and as he said it, the sovereigns clinked in his mouth.

"Ah! You rascal! Then you have hidden your money under your tongue! Spit it out at once!"

But Pinocchio was obdurate.

"Ah! You pretend to be deaf, do you? Wait a moment, leave it to us to find a means to make you spit it out."

And one of them seized the puppet by the end of his nose, and the other took him by the chin, and began to pull them brutally, the one up and the other down, to constrain him to open his mouth. But it was all to no purpose. Pinocchio's mouth seemed to be nailed and riveted together.

Then the shorter assassin drew out an ugly knife and tried to force it between his lips like a lever or chisel. But Pinocchio, as quick as lightning, caught his hand with his teeth, and with one bite bit it clean off and spat it out. Imagine his astonishment when instead of a hand he perceived that he had spat a cat's paw to the ground.

Encouraged by his first victory he used his nails to such purpose that he succeeded in liberating himself from his assailants, and jumping the hedge by the roadside he began to fly across the country. The assassins ran after him like two dogs chasing a hare; and the one who had lost a paw ran on one leg, and no one ever knew how he managed it.

After a race of some miles Pinocchio could do no more. Giving himself up for lost he climbed the stem of a very high pine tree and seated himself in the top-most branches. The assassins attempted to climb after him, but when they had reached halfway up the stem they slid down again, and arrived on the ground with the skin grazed from their hands and knees.

But they were not to be beaten by so little: collecting a quantity of dry wood they piled it beneath the pine and set fire to it. In less time than it takes to tell, the pine began to burn and to flame like a candle blown by the wind. Pinocchio, seeing that the flames were mounting higher every instant, and not wishing to end his life like a roasted pigeon, made a stupendous leap from the top of the tree

and started afresh across the fields and vineyards. The assassins followed him, and kept behind him without once
giving in.

The day began to break and they were still pursuing
him. Suddenly Pinocchio found his way barred by a wide
deep ditch full of dirty water the color of coffee. What was
he to do? "One! two! three!" cried the puppet, and making
a rush he sprang to the other side. The assassins also
jumped, but not having measured the distance properly,
splash, splash! they fell into the very middle of the ditch.
Pinocchio, who heard the plunge and the splashing of the
water, shouted out, laughing, and without stopping:

"A fine bath to you, gentlemen assassins."

And he felt convinced that they were drowned, when,
turning to look, he perceived that on the contrary they
were both running after him, still enveloped in their sacks,
with the water dripping from them as if they had been two
hollow baskets.

Chapter XV

The assassins pursue PINOCCHIO; *and having overtaken him hang him to a branch of the Big Oak*

At this sight the puppet's courage failed him, and he was on the point of throwing himself on the ground and giving himself over for lost. Turning, however, his eyes in every direction, he saw at some distance, standing out amidst the dark green of the trees, a small house as white as snow.

"If I had only breath to reach that house," he said to himself, "perhaps I should be saved."

And without delaying an instant, he recommenced running for his life through the wood, and the assassins after him.

At last, after a desperate race of nearly two hours, he arrived quite breathless at the door of the house, and knocked.

No one answered.

He knocked again with great violence, for he heard the sound of steps approaching him, and the heavy panting of his persecutors. The same silence.

Seeing that knocking was useless he began in desperation to kick and pommel the door with all his might. The window then opened and a beautiful Child appeared at it. She had blue hair and a face as white as a waxen image; her eyes were closed and her hands were crossed on her breast. Without moving her lips in the least, she said in a voice that seemed to come from the other world:

"In this house there is no one. They are all dead."

"Then at least open the door for me yourself," shouted Pinocchio, crying and imploring.

"I am dead also."

"Dead? Then what are you doing there at the window?"

"I am waiting for the bier to come to carry me away."

Having said this she immediately disappeared, and the window was closed again without the slightest noise.

"Oh, beautiful Child with blue hair," cried Pinocchio, "open the door for pity's sake! Have compassion on a poor boy pursued by assas . . ."

But he could not finish the word, for he felt himself seized by the collar, and the same two horrible voices said to him threateningly:

"You shall not escape from us again!"

The puppet, seeing death staring him in the face, was taken with such a violent fit of trembling that the joints of his wooden legs began to creak, and the sovereigns hidden under his tongue to clink.

"Now then," demanded the assassins, "will you open your mouth, yes or no? Ah; no answer? . . . Leave it to us: this time we will force you to open it!"

And drawing out two long horrid knives as sharp as razors, clash! they attempted to stab him twice.

But the puppet, luckily for him, was made of very hard wood; the knives therefore broke into a thousand pieces, and the assassins were left with the handles in their hands staring at each other.

"I see what we must do," said one of them. "He must be hung; let us hang him!"

"Let us hang him!" repeated the other.

Without loss of time they tied his arms behind him,

passed a running noose round his throat, and then hung him to the branch of a tree called the Big Oak.

They then sat down on the grass and waited for his last struggle. But at the end of three hours the puppet's eyes were still open, his mouth closed, and he was kicking more than ever.

Losing patience, they turned to Pinocchio and said in a bantering tone:

"Good-by till tomorrow. Let us hope that when we return you will be polite enough to allow yourself to be found quite dead, and with your mouth wide open."

And they walked off.

In the meantime a tempestuous northerly wind began to blow and roar angrily, and it beat the poor puppet as he hung, from side to side, making him swing violently like the clatter of a bell ringing for a wedding. And the swinging gave him atrocious spasms, and the running noose, becoming still tighter round his throat, took away his breath.

Little by little his eyes began to grow dim, but although he felt that death was near he still continued to hope that some charitable person would come to his assistance before it was too late. But when, after waiting and waiting, he found that no one came, absolutely no one, then he remembered his poor father, and thinking he was dying, he stammered out:

"Oh, Papa, Papa! If only you were here!"

His breath failed him and he could say no more. He shut his eyes, opened his mouth, stretched his legs, gave a long shudder, and hung stiff and insensible.

Chapter XVI

The beautiful CHILD *with blue hair has the puppet taken down; has him put to bed and calls in three doctors to know if he is alive or dead*

While poor Pinocchio, suspended to a branch of the Big Oak, was apparently more dead than alive, the beautiful Child with blue hair came again to the window. When she saw the unhappy puppet hanging by his throat, and dancing up and down in the gusts of the north wind, she was moved by compassion. Striking her hands together she made three little claps.

At this signal there came a sound of the sweep of wings flying rapidly, and a large Falcon flew on to the window sill.

"What are your orders, gracious Fairy?" he asked, inclining his beak in sign of reverence—for I must tell you that the Child with blue hair was no more and no less than a beautiful Fairy, who for more than a thousand years had lived in the wood.

"Do you see that puppet dangling from a branch of the Big Oak?"

"I see him."

"Very well. Fly there at once: with your strong beak

break the knot that keeps him suspended in the air, and lay him gently on the grass at the foot of the tree."

The Falcon flew away, and after two minutes he returned, saying:

"I have done as you commanded."

"And how did you find him?"

"To see him he appeared dead, but he cannot really be quite dead, for I had no sooner loosened the running noose that tightened his throat than, giving a sigh, he muttered in a faint voice: 'Now I feel better!' . . ."

The Fairy, then striking her hands together, made two little claps, and a magnificent Poodle appeared, walking upright on his hind legs exactly as if he had been a man.

He was in the full-dress livery of a coachman. On his head he had a three-cornered cap braided with gold, his curly white wig came down onto his shoulders, he had a chocolate-colored waistcoat with diamond buttons, and two large pockets to contain the bones that his mistress gave him at dinner. He had besides a pair of short crimson velvet breeches, silk stockings, cut-down shoes, and hanging behind him a species of umbrella case made of blue satin, to put his tail into when the weather was rainy.

"Be quick, Medoro, like a good dog!" said the Fairy to the Poodle. "Have the most beautiful carriage in my coach house put to, and take the road to the wood. When you come to the Big Oak you will find a poor puppet stretched on the grass half dead. Pick him up gently, and lay him flat on the cushions of the carriage and bring him here to me. Have you understood?"

The Poodle, to show that he had understood, shook the case of blue satin three or four times, and ran off like a race horse.

Shortly afterward a beautiful little carriage came out of the coach house. The cushions were stuffed with canary feathers, and it was lined in the inside with whipped cream, custard, and Savoy biscuits. The little carriage was drawn by a hundred pairs of white mice, and the Poodle, seated on the coach box, cracked his whip from side to side like a driver when he is afraid that he is behind time.

A quarter of an hour had not passed when the carriage returned. The Fairy, who was waiting at the door of the house, took the poor puppet in her arms, and carried him into a little room that was wainscoted with mother-of-pearl, and sent at once to summon the most famous doctors in the neighborhood.

The doctors came immediately one after another: namely, a Crow, an Owl, and a Talking Cricket.

"I wish to know from you gentlemen," said the Fairy, turning to the three doctors who were assembled round Pinocchio's bed—"I wish to know from you gentlemen, if this unfortunate puppet is alive or dead!"

At this request the Crow, advancing first, felt Pinocchio's pulse; then he felt his nose, and then the little toe of his foot: and having done this carefully, he pronounced solemnly the following words:

"To my belief the puppet is already quite dead; but if fortunately he should not be dead, then it would be a sign that he is still alive!"

"I regret," said the Owl, "to be obliged to contradict the Crow, my illustrious friend and colleague; but in my opinion the puppet is still alive: but if unfortunately he should not be alive, then it would be a sign that he is dead indeed!"

"And you—have you nothing to say?" asked the Fairy of the Talking Cricket.

"In my opinion the wisest thing a prudent doctor can do, when he does not know what he is talking about, is to be silent. For the rest, that puppet there has a face that is not new to me. I have known him for some time! . . ."

Pinocchio, who up to that moment had lain immovable, like a real piece of wood, was seized with a fit of convulsive trembling that shook the whole bed.

"That puppet there," continued the Talking Cricket, "is a confirmed rogue."

Pinocchio opened his eyes, but shut them again immediately.

"He is a ragamuffin, a do-nothing, a vagabond."

Pinocchio hid his face beneath the clothes.

"That puppet there is a disobedient son who will make his poor father die of a broken heart!"

At that instant a suffocated sound of sobs and crying was heard in the room. Imagine everybody's astonishment when, having raised the sheets a little, it was discovered that the sounds came from Pinocchio.

"When the dead person cries, it is a sign that he is on the road to get well," said the Crow solemnly.

"I grieve to contradict my illustrious friend and colleague," added the Owl, "but for me, when the dead person cries, it is a sign that he is sorry to die."

Chapter XVII

PINOCCHIO *eats the sugar, but will not take his medicine; when, however, he sees the gravediggers, who have arrived to carry him away, he takes it. He then tells a lie, and as a punishment his nose grows longer*

As soon as the three doctors had left the room the Fairy approached Pinocchio, and having touched his forehead she perceived that he was in a high fever that was not to be trifled with.

She therefore dissolved a certain white powder in half a tumbler of water, and offering it to the puppet she said to him lovingly:

"Drink it, and in a few days you will be cured."

Pinocchio looked at the tumbler, made a wry face, and then asked in a plaintive voice:

"Is it sweet or bitter?"

"It is bitter, but it will do you good."

"If it is bitter, I will not take it."

"Listen to me: drink it."

"I don't like anything bitter."

"Drink it, and when you have drunk it I will give you a lump of sugar to take away the taste."

"Where is the lump of sugar?"

"Here it is," said the Fairy, taking a piece from a gold sugar basin.

"Give me first the lump of sugar, and then I will drink that bad bitter water."

"Do you promise me?"

"Yes."

The Fairy gave him the sugar, and Pinocchio having crunched it up and swallowed it in a second, said, licking his lips:

"It would be a fine thing if sugar were medicine! I would take it every day."

"Now keep your promise and drink these few drops of water, which will restore you to health."

Pinocchio took the tumbler unwillingly in his hand and put the point of his nose to it: he then approached it to his lips: he then again put his nose to it, and at last said:

"It is too bitter, too bitter! I cannot drink it."

"How can you tell that, when you have not even tasted it?"

"I can imagine it! I know it from the smell. I want first another lump of sugar ... and then I will drink it!"

The Fairy then, with all the patience of a good mamma, put another lump of sugar in his mouth, and then again presented the tumbler to him.

"I cannot drink it so!" said the puppet, making a thousand grimaces.

"Why?"

"Because that pillow that is down there on my feet bothers me."

The Fairy removed the pillow.

"It is useless. Even so I cannot drink it."

"What is the matter now?"

"The door of the room, which is half open, bothers me."

The Fairy went and closed the door.

"In short," cried Pinocchio, bursting into tears, "I will not drink that bitter water—no, no, no!"

"My boy, you will repent it."

"I don't care."

"Your illness is serious."

"I don't care."

"The fever in a few hours will carry you into the other world."

"I don't care."

"Are you not afraid of death?"

"I am not in the least afraid! I would rather die than drink that bitter medicine."

At that moment the door of the room flew open, and four rabbits as black as ink entered carrying on their shoulders a little bier.

"What do you want with me?" cried Pinocchio, sitting up in bed in a great fright.

"We are come to take you," said the biggest rabbit.

"To take me? . . . But I am not yet dead!"

"No, not yet: but you have only a few minutes to live, as you have refused the medicine that would have cured you of the fever."

"Oh, Fairy, Fairy!" the puppet then began to scream. "Give me the tumbler at once . . . be quick, for pity's sake, for I will not die—no . . . I will not die. . . ."

And taking the tumbler in both hands he emptied it at a draught.

"We must have patience!" said the rabbits. "This time we have made our journey in vain." And taking the little bier again on their shoulders they left the room, grumbling and murmuring between their teeth.

In fact, a few minutes afterward Pinocchio jumped down from the bed quite well: because you must know that wooden puppets have the privilege of being seldom ill and of being cured very quickly.

The Fairy, seeing him running and rushing about the

room as gay and as lively as a young cock, said to
him:

"Then my medicine has really done you good?"

"Good, I should think so! It has restored me to
life!"

"Then why on earth did you require so much persuasion
to take it?"

"Because, you see, we boys are all like that! We are
more afraid of medicine than of the illness."

"Disgraceful! Boys ought to know that a good remedy
taken in time may save them from a serious illness, and
perhaps even from death."

"Oh, but another time I shall not require so much persuasion. I shall remember those black rabbits with the bier
on their shoulders ... and then I shall immediately take
the tumbler in my hand, and down it will go!"

"Now come here to me, and tell me how it came about
that you fell into the hands of those assassins."

"It came about that the showman Fire-eater gave me
some gold pieces and said to me: 'Go, and take them to
your father!' and instead I met on the road a Fox and a
Cat, two very respectable persons, who said to me: 'Would
you like those pieces of gold to become a thousand or
two? Come with us and we will take you to the Field of
Miracles,' and I said: 'Let us go.' And they said: 'Let us
stop at the inn of the Red Crawfish,' and before midnight
they left. And when I awoke I found that they were no
longer there, because they had gone away. Then I began to
travel by night, for you cannot imagine how dark it was;
and on that account I met on the road two assassins in
charcoal sacks who said to me: 'Out with your money,'
and I said to them: 'I have got none,' because I had hidden
the four gold pieces in my mouth, and one of the assassins
tried to put his hand in my mouth, and I bit his hand off
and spat it out, but instead of a hand I spat out a cat's paw.
And the assassins ran after me, and I ran, and ran, until at
last they caught me, and tied me by the neck to a tree in

this wood, and said to me: 'Tomorrow we shall return here, and then you will be dead with your mouth open, and we shall be able to carry off the pieces of gold that you have hidden under your tongue.' "

"And the four pieces—where have you put them?" asked the fairy.

"I have lost them!" said Pinocchio; but he was telling a lie, for he had them in his pocket.

He had scarcely told the lie when his nose, which was already long, grew at once two fingers longer.

"And where did you lose them?"

"In the wood near here."

At this second lie his nose went on growing.

"If you have lost them in the wood near here," said the Fairy, "we will look for them, and we shall find them: because everything that is lost in that wood is always found."

"Ah! Now I remember all about it," replied the puppet, getting quite confused. "I didn't lose the four gold pieces, I swallowed them inadvertently while I was drinking your medicine."

At this third lie his nose grew to such an extraordinary length that poor Pinocchio could not move in any direction. If he turned to one side he struck his nose against the bed or the windowpanes, if he turned to the other he struck it against the walls or the door, if he raised his head a little he ran the risk of sticking it into one of the Fairy's eyes.

And the Fairy looked at him and laughed.

"What are you laughing at?" asked the puppet, very confused and anxious at finding his nose growing so prodigiously.

"I am laughing at the lie you have told."

"And how can you possibly know that I have told a lie?"

"Lies, my dear boy, are found out immediately, because they are of two sorts. There are lies that have short legs, and lies that have long noses. Your lie, as it happens, is one of those that have a long nose."

Pinocchio, not knowing where to hide himself for shame, tried to run out of the room; but he did not succeed, for his nose had increased so much that it could no longer pass through the door.

Chapter XVIII

The Fairy, as you can imagine, allowed the puppet to cry and to roar for a good half hour over his nose, which could no longer pass through the door of the room. This she did to give him a severe lesson, and to correct him of the disgraceful fault of telling lies—the most disgraceful fault that a boy can have. But when she saw him quite disfigured, and his eyes swollen out of his head from weeping, she felt full of compassion for him. She therefore beat her hands together, and at that signal a thousand large birds called Woodpeckers flew in at the window. They immediately perched on Pinocchio's nose, and began to peck at it with such zeal that in a few minutes his enormous and ridiculous nose was reduced to its usual dimensions.

"What a good Fairy you are," said the puppet, drying his eyes, "and how much I love you!"

"I love you also," answered the Fairy, "and if you will remain with me, you shall be my little brother and I will be your good little sister."

"I would remain willingly ... but my poor papa?"

"I have thought of everything. I have already let your father know, and he will be here tonight."

"Really?" shouted Pinocchio, jumping for joy. "Then, little Fairy, if you consent, I should like to go and meet him. I am so anxious to give a kiss to that poor old man, who has suffered so much on my account, that I am counting the minutes."

"Go, then, but be careful not to lose yourself. Take the road through the wood and I am sure that you will meet him."

Pinocchio set out; and as soon as he was in the wood he began to run like a kid. But when he had reached a certain spot, almost in front of the Big Oak, he stopped, because he thought that he heard people among the bushes. In fact, two persons came out onto the road. Can you guess who they were? . . . His two traveling companions, the Fox and the Cat, with whom he had supped at the inn of the Red Crawfish.

"Why, here is our dear Pinocchio!" cried the Fox, kissing and embracing him. "How come you to be here?"

"How come you to be here?" repeated the Cat.

"It is a long story," answered the puppet, "which I will tell you when I have time. But do you know that the other night, when you left me alone at the inn, I met with assassins on the road."

"Assassins! . . . Oh, poor Pinocchio! And what did they want?"

"They wanted to rob me of my gold pieces."

"Villains!" said the fox.

"Infamous villains!" repeated the Cat.

"But I ran away from them," continued the puppet, "and they followed me. And at last they overtook me and hung me to a branch of that oak tree."

And Pinocchio pointed to the Big Oak, which was two steps from them.

"Is it possible to hear of anything more dreadful?" said the Fox. "In what a world we are condemned to live! Where can respectable people like us find a safe refuge?"

While they were thus talking Pinocchio observed that the Cat was lame of her front right leg, for in fact she had lost her paw with all its claws. He therefore asked her:

"What have you done with your paw?"

The Cat tried to answer but became confused. Therefore the Fox said immediately:

"My friend is too modest, and that is why she doesn't speak. I will answer for her. I must tell you that an hour ago we met an old wolf on the road, almost fainting from want of food, who asked alms of us. Not having so much as a fishbone to give him, what did my friend, who has really the heart of a Caesar, do? She bit off one of her forepaws, and threw it to that poor beast that he might appease his hunger."

And the fox, in relating this, dried a tear.

Pinocchio also was touched, and approaching the Cat he whispered into her ear:

"If all cats resembled you, how fortunate the mice would be!"

"And now, what are you doing here?" asked the Fox of the puppet.

"I am waiting for my papa, whom I expect to arrive any moment."

"And your gold pieces?"

"I have got them in my pocket, all but one that I spent at the inn of the Red Crawfish."

"And to think that, instead of four pieces, by tomorrow they might become one or two thousand! Why do you not listen to my advice? Why will you not go and bury them in the Field of Miracles?"

"Today it is impossible: I will go another day."

"Another day will be too late!" said the Fox.

"Why?"

"Because the field has been bought by a gentleman, and after tomorrow no one will be allowed to bury money there."

"How far off is the Field of Miracles?"

"Not two miles. Will you come with us? In half an hour

you will be there. You can bury your money at once, and
in a few minutes you will collect two thousand, and this
evening you will return with your pockets full. Will you
come with us?"

Pinocchio thought of the good Fairy, old Geppetto, and
the warnings of the Talking Cricket, and he hesitated a little before answering. He ended, however, by doing as all
boys do who have not a grain of sense and who have no
heart—he ended by giving his head a little shake, and saying to the Fox and the Cat:

"Let us go: I will come with you."

And they went.

After having walked half the day they reached a town
that was called "Trap for Blockheads." As soon as Pinocchio entered this town, he saw that the streets were
crowded with dogs who had lost their coats and who were
yawning from hunger, shorn sheep trembling with cold,
cocks without combs or crests who were begging for a
grain of Indian corn, large butterflies who could no longer
fly because they had sold their beautiful colored wings,
peacocks who had no tails and were ashamed to be seen,
and pheasants who went scratching about in a subdued
fashion, mourning for their brilliant gold and silver feathers gone forever.

In the midst of this crowd of beggars and shame-faced
creatures, some lordly carriage passed from time to time
containing a Fox, or a thieving Magpie, or some other ravenous bird of prey.

"And where is the Field of Miracles?" asked Pinocchio.

"It is here, not two steps from us."

They crossed the town, and having gone beyond the
walls they came to a solitary field which to look at resembled all other fields.

"We are arrived," said the Fox to the puppet. "Now
stoop down and dig with your hands a little hole in the
ground and put your gold pieces into it."

Pinocchio obeyed. He dug a hole, put into it the four

gold pieces that he had left, and then filled up the hole with a little earth.

"Now, then," said the Fox, "go to that canal close to us, fetch a can of water, and water the ground where you have sowed them."

Pinocchio went to the canal, and as he had no can he took off one of his old shoes, and filling it with water he watered the ground over the hole.

He then asked:

"Is there anything else to be done?"

"Nothing else," answered the Fox. "We can now go away. You can return in about twenty minutes, and you will find a shrub already pushing through the ground, with its branches quite loaded with money."

The poor puppet, beside himself with joy, thanked the Fox and the Cat a thousand times, and promised them a beautiful present.

"We wish for no presents," answered the two rascals. "It is enough for us to have taught you the way to enrich yourself without undergoing hard work, and we are as happy as folk out for a holiday."

Thus saying they took leave of Pinocchio, and, wishing him a good harvest, went about their business.

Chapter XIX

PINOCCHIO *is robbed of his money, and as a punishment he is sent to prison for four months*

The puppet returned to the town and began to count the minutes one by one; and when he thought that it must be time he took the road leading to the Field of Miracles.

And as he walked along with hurried steps his heart beat fast tic, tac, tic, tac, like a drawing-room clock when it is really going well. Meanwhile he was thinking to himself:

"And if instead of a thousand gold pieces, I was to find on the branches of the tree two thousand? And instead of two thousand supposing I found five thousand? And instead of five thousand that I found a hundred thousand? Oh, what a fine gentleman I should then become! ... I would have a beautiful palace, a thousand little wooden horses and a thousand stables to amuse myself with, a cellar full of currant wine and sweet syrups, and a library quite full of candies, tarts, plum cakes, macaroons, and biscuits with cream."

While he was building these castles in the air he had arrived in the neighborhood of the field, and he stopped to look if by chance he could perceive a tree with its branches laden with money: but he saw nothing. He advanced another hundred steps—nothing: he entered the field . . . he went right up to the little hole where he had buried his sovereigns—and nothing. He then became very thoughtful, and forgetting the rules of society and good manners he took his hands out of his pockets and gave his head a long scratch.

At that moment he heard an explosion of laughter close to him, and looking up he saw a large Parrot perched on a tree, who was preening the few feathers he had left.

"Why are you laughing?" asked Pinocchio in an angry voice.

"I am laughing because in preening my feathers I tickled myself under my wings."

The puppet did not answer, but went to the canal and, filling the same old shoe full of water, he proceeded to water the earth afresh that covered his gold pieces.

While he was thus occupied another laugh, and still more impertinent than the first, rang out in the silence of that solitary place.

"Once for all," shouted Pinocchio in a rage, "may I know, you ill-educated Parrot, what you are laughing at?"

"I am laughing at those simpletons who believe in all the foolish things that are told them, and who allow themselves to be entrapped by those who are more cunning than they are."

"Are you perhaps speaking of me?"

"Yes, I am speaking of you, poor Pinocchio—of you who are simple enough to believe that money can be sown and gathered in fields in the same way as beans and gourds. I also believed it once, and today I am suffering for it. Today—but it is too late—I have learned at last that to put a few pennies honestly together it is necessary to know how to earn them, either by the work of our own hands or by the cleverness of our own brains."

"I don't understand you," said the puppet, who was already trembling with fear.

"Have patience! I will explain myself better," rejoined the Parrot. "You must know, then, that while you were in the town the Fox and the Cat returned to the field: they took the buried money and then fled like the wind. And now he that catches them will be clever."

Pinocchio remained with his mouth open, and not choosing to believe the Parrot's words he began with his hands and nails to dig up the earth that he had watered. And he dug, and dug, and dug, and made such a deep hole that a rick of straw might have stood upright in it: but the money was no longer there.

He rushed back to the town in a state of desperation and went at once to the Courts of Justice to denounce the two knaves who had robbed him to the judge.

The judge was a big ape of the gorilla tribe—an old ape respectable for his age, his white beard, but especially for his gold spectacles without glasses that he was always obliged to wear, on account of an inflammation of the eyes that had tormented him for many years.

Pinocchio related in the presence of the judge all the particulars of the infamous fraud of which he had been the victim. He gave the names, the surnames, and other details, of the two rascals, and ended by demanding justice.

The judge listened with great benignity; took a lively interest in the story; was much touched and moved; and when the puppet had nothing further to say, he stretched out his hand and rang a bell.

At this summons two mastiffs immediately appeared dressed as gendarmes. The judge then, pointing to Pinocchio, said to them:

"That poor devil has been robbed of four gold pieces; take him up, and put him immediately into prison."

The puppet was petrified on hearing this unexpected sentence, and tried to protest; but the gendarmes, to avoid losing time, stopped his mouth, and carried him off to the lockup.

And there he remained for four months—four long months—and he would have remained longer still if a fortunate chance had not released him. For I must tell you that the young Emperor who reigned over the town of Trap for Blockheads, having won a splendid victory over his enemies, ordered great public rejoicings. There were illuminations, fireworks, horse races, and velocipede races, and as a further sign of triumph he commanded that the prisons should be opened and all the prisoners liberated.

"If the others are to be let out of prison, I will go also," said Pinocchio to the jailer.

"No, not you," said the jailer, "because you do not belong to the fortunate class."

"I beg your pardon," replied Pinocchio, "I am also a criminal."

"In that case you are perfectly right," said the jailer; and taking off his hat and bowing to him respectfully he opened the prison doors and let him escape.

Chapter XX

Liberated from prison, he starts to return to the FAIRY'S *house, but on the road he meets with a horrible* SERPENT, *and afterwards he is caught in a trap*

You can imagine Pinocchio's joy when he found himself free. Without stopping to take breath he immediately left the town and took the road that led to the Fairy's house.

On account of the rainy weather the road had become a marsh into which he sank knee-deep. But the puppet would not give in. Tormented by the desire of seeing his father and his little sister with blue hair again he ran and leapt like a greyhound, and as he ran he was splashed with mud from head to foot. And he said to himself as he went along: "How many misfortunes have happened to me . . . and I deserved them; for I am an obstinate, passionate puppet. . . . I am always bent upon having my own way, without listening to those who wish me well, and who have a thousand times more sense than I have! . . . But from this time forth I am determined to change and to become orderly and obedient. . . . For at last I have seen that disobedient boys come to no good and gain nothing. And will Papa have waited for me? Shall I find him at the

Fairy's house! Poor man, it is so long since I last saw him: I am dying to embrace him, and to cover him with kisses! And will the Fairy forgive me my bad conduct to her? ... To think of all the kindness and loving care I received from her ... to think that if I am now alive I owe it to her! ... Would it be possible to find a more ungrateful boy, or one with less heart than I have! ..."

While he was saying this he stopped suddenly, frightened to death, and made four steps backwards.

What had he seen? ...

He had seen an immense Serpent stretched across the road. Its skin was green, it had red eyes, and a pointed tail that was smoking like a chimney.

It would be impossible to imagine the puppet's terror. He walked away to a safe distance, and sitting down on a heap of stones waited until the Serpent should have gone about its business and had left the road clear.

He waited an hour; two hours; three hours; but the Serpent was always there, and even from a distance he could see the light of his fiery eyes and the column of smoke that ascended from the end of his tail.

At last Pinocchio, trying to feel courageous, approached to within a few steps, and said to the Serpent in a little soft, insinuating voice:

"Excuse me, Sir Serpent, but would you be so good as to move a little to one side, just enough to allow me to pass?"

He might as well have spoken to the wall. Nobody moved.

He began again in the same soft voice:

"You must know, Sir Serpent, that I am on my way home, where my father is waiting for me, and it is such a long time since I saw him last! ... Will you therefore allow me to continue my road?"

He waited for a sign in answer to this request, but there was none: in fact the Serpent, who up to that moment had been sprightly and full of life, became motionless and almost rigid. He shut his eyes and his tail ceased smoking.

"Can he really be dead?" said Pinocchio, rubbing his hands with delight; and he determined to jump over him and reach the other side of the road. But just as he was going to leap, the Serpent raised himself suddenly on end, like a spring set in motion; and the puppet, drawing back, in his terror caught his feet and fell to the ground.

And he fell so awkwardly that his head stuck in the mud and his legs went into the air.

At the sight of the puppet kicking violently with his head in the mud the Serpent went into convulsions of laughter, and he laughed, and laughed, and laughed, until from the violence of his laughter he broke a blood vessel in his chest and died. And that time he was really dead.

Pinocchio then set off running in hope that he should reach the Fairy's house before dark. But before long he began to suffer so dreadfully from hunger that he could not bear it, and he jumped into a field by the wayside intending to pick some bunches of muscatel grapes. Oh, that he had never done it!

He had scarcely reached the vines when crac! ... his legs were caught between two cutting iron bars, and he became so giddy with pain that stars of every color danced before his eyes.

The poor puppet had been taken in a trap put there to capture some big polecats who were the scourge of the poultry yards in the neighborhood.

Chapter XXI

PINOCCHIO *is taken by a peasant, who obliges him to fill the place of his watchdog in the poultry yard*

Pinocchio, as you can imagine, began to cry and scream: but his tears and groans were useless, for there was not a house to be seen, and not a living soul passed down the road.

At last night came on.

Partly from the pain of the trap that cut his legs, and a little from fear at finding himself alone in the dark in the midst of the fields, the puppet was on the point of fainting. Just at that moment he saw a Firefly flitting over his head. He called to it and said:

"Oh, little Firefly, will you have pity on me and liberate me from this torture?"

"Poor boy!" said the Firefly, stopping and looking at him with compassion. "But how could your legs have been caught by those sharp irons?"

"I came into the field to pick two bunches of these muscatel grapes, and. . . ."

"But were the grapes yours?"

"No."

"Then who taught you to carry off other people's property?"

"I was so hungry."

"Hunger, my boy, is not a good reason for appropriating what does not belong to us."

"That is true, that is true!" said Pinocchio, crying. "I will never do it again."

At this moment their conversation was interrupted by a slight sound of approaching footsteps. It was the owner of the field coming on tiptoe to see if one of the polecats that ate his chickens during the night had been caught in his trap.

His astonishment was great when, having brought out his lantern from under his coat, he perceived that instead of a polecat a boy had been taken.

"Ah, little thief," said the angry peasant, "then it is you who carry off my chickens?"

"No, it is not I; indeed it is not!" cried Pinocchio, sobbing. "I only came into the field to take two bunches of grapes!"

"He who steals grapes is quite capable of stealing chickens. Leave it to me, I will give you a lesson that you will not forget in a hurry."

Opening the trap he seized the puppet by the collar, and carried him to his house as if he had been a young lamb.

When he reached the yard in front of the house he threw him roughly on the ground, and putting his foot on his neck he said to him:

"It is late, and I want to go to bed; we will settle our accounts tomorrow. In the meanwhile, as the dog who kept guard at night died today, you shall take his place at once. You shall be my watchdog."

And taking a great collar covered with brass knobs he strapped it tightly round Pinocchio's throat that he might not be able to draw his head out of it. A heavy chain attached to the collar was fastened to the wall.

"If it should rain tonight," he then said to him, "you can go and lie down in the kennel; the straw that has served as a bed for my poor dog for the last four years is still there. If unfortunately robbers should come, remember to keep your ears pricked and to bark."

After giving him this last injunction the man went into the house, shut the door, and put up the chain.

Poor Pinocchio remained lying on the ground more dead than alive from the effects of cold, hunger, and fear. From time to time he put his hands angrily to the collar that tightened his throat and said, crying:

"It serves me right! Decidedly it serves me right! I was determined to be a vagabond and a good-for-nothing. I would listen to bad companions, and that is why I always meet with misfortunes. If I had been a good little boy as so many are; if I had been willing to learn and to work; if I had remained at home with my poor papa, I should not now be in the midst of the fields and obliged to be the watchdog to a peasant's house. Oh, if I could be born again! But now it is too late, and I must have patience!"

Relieved by this little outburst, which came straight from his heart, he went into the dog kennel and fell asleep.

Chapter XXII

He had been sleeping heavily for about two hours when, toward midnight, he was roused by a whispering of strange voices that seemed to come from the courtyard. Putting the point of his nose out of the kennel he saw four little beasts with dark fur, that looked like cats, standing consulting together. But they were not cats; they were polecats—carnivorous little animals, especially greedy for eggs and young chickens. One of the polecats, leaving his companions, came to the opening of the kennel and said in a low voice:

"Good evening, Melampo."

"My name is not Melampo," answered the puppet.

"Oh! Then, who are you?"

"I am Pinocchio."

"And what are you doing here?"

"I am acting as watchdog."

"Then where is Melampo? Where is the old dog who lived in this kennel?"

"He died this morning."

"Is he dead? Poor beast! He was so good. But judging you by your face I should say that you were also a good dog."

"I beg your pardon, I am not a dog."

"Not a dog? Then, what are you?"

"I am a puppet."

"And you are acting as watchdog?"

"That is only too true—as a punishment."

"Well, then, I will offer you the same conditions that we made with the deceased Melampo, and I am sure you will be satisfied with them."

"What are these conditions?"

"One night in every week you are to permit us to visit this poultry yard as we have hitherto done, and to carry off eight chickens. Of these chickens seven are to be eaten by us, and one we will give to you, on the express understanding, however, that you pretend to be asleep, and that it never enters your head to bark and to wake the peasant."

"Did Melampo act in this manner?" asked Pinocchio.

"Certainly, and we were always on the best terms with him. Sleep quietly, and rest assured that before we go we will leave by the kennel a beautiful chicken ready plucked for your breakfast tomorrow. Have we understood each other clearly?"

"Only too clearly! . . ." answered Pinocchio, and he shook his head threateningly as much as to say: "You shall hear of this shortly!"

The four polecats, thinking themselves safe, repaired to the poultry yard, which was close to the kennel, and having opened the wooden gate with their teeth and claws, they slipped in one by one. But they had only just passed through when they heard the gate shut behind them with great violence.

It was Pinocchio who had shut it; and for greater security he put a large stone against it to keep it closed.

He then began to bark, and he barked exactly like a watchdog: bow-wow, bow-wow.

Hearing the barking the peasant jumped out of bed, and taking his gun he came to the window and asked:

"What is the matter?"

"There are robbers!" answered Pinocchio.

"Where are they?"

"In the poultry yard."

"I will come down directly."

In fact, in less time than it takes to say Amen, the peasant came down. He rushed into the poultry yard, caught the polecats, and having put them into a sack, he said to them in a tone of great satisfaction:

"At last you have fallen into my hands! I might punish you, but I am not so cruel. I will content myself instead by carrying you in the morning to the innkeeper of the neighboring village, who will skin and cook you as hares with a sweet and sour sauce. It is an honor that you don't deserve, but generous people like me don't consider such trifles!"

He then approached Pinocchio and began to caress him, and among other things he asked him:

"How did you manage to discover the four thieves? To think that Melampo, my faithful Melampo, never found out anything!"

The puppet might then have told him the whole story; he might have informed him of the disgraceful conditions that had been made between the dog and the polecats; but he remembered that the dog was dead, and he thought to himself:

"What is the good of accusing the dead? . . . The dead are dead, and the best thing to be done is to leave them in peace!"

"When the thieves got into the yard were you asleep or awake?" the peasant went on to ask him.

"I was asleep," answered Pinocchio, "but the polecats woke me with their chatter, and one of them came to the kennel and said to me: 'If you promise not to bark, and not to wake the master, we will make you a present of a fine chicken ready plucked!' To think that they should have the audacity to make such a proposal to me! For although I am a puppet, possessing perhaps nearly all the faults in the world, there is one that I certainly will never be guilty of, that of making terms with, and sharing the gains of, dishonest people!"

"Well said, my boy!" cried the peasant, slapping him on the shoulder. "Such sentiments do you honor; and as a proof of my gratitude I will at once set you at liberty, and you may return home."

And he removed the dog collar.

Chapter XXIII

PINOCCHIO *mourns the death of the beautiful* CHILD *with the blue hair. He then meets with a* PIGEON *who flies with him to the seashore, and there he throws himself into the water to go to the assistance of his father,* GEPPETTO

As soon as Pinocchio was released from the heavy and humiliating weight of the dog collar he started across the fields, and never stopped until he had reached the highroad that led to the Fairy's house. There he turned and looked down into the plain beneath. He could see distinctly with his naked eye the wood where he had been so unfortunate as to meet with the Fox and the Cat; he could see among the trees the top of the Big Oak to which he had been hung; but although he looked in every direction, the little house belonging to the beautiful Child with the blue hair was nowhere visible.

Seized with a sad presentiment he began to run with all the strength he had left, and in a few minutes he reached the field where the little white house had once stood. But the little white house was no longer there. He saw instead a marble stone, on which were engraved these sad words:

HERE LIES
THE CHILD WITH THE BLUE HAIR
WHO DIED FROM SORROW
BECAUSE SHE WAS ABANDONED BY HER
LITTLE BROTHER PINOCCHIO

I leave you to imagine the puppet's feelings when he had with difficulty spelled out this epitaph. He fell with his face on the ground and, covering the tombstone with a thousand kisses, burst into an agony of tears. He cried all night, and when morning came he was still crying although he had no tears left, and his sobs and lamentations were so acute and heartbreaking that they roused the echoes in the surrounding hills.

And as he wept he said:

"Oh, little Fairy, why did you die? Why did not I die instead of you, I who am so wicked, while you were so good? ... And my papa? Where can he be? Oh, little Fairy, tell me where I can find him, for I want to remain with him always and never to leave him again, never again! ... Oh, little Fairy, tell me that it is not true that you are dead! ... If you really love me ... if you really love your little brother, come to life again ... come to life as you were before! ... Does it not grieve you to see me alone and abandoned by everybody? ... If assassins come they will hang me again to the branch of a tree ... and then I should die indeed. What do you imagine that I can do here alone in the world? Now that I have lost you and my papa, who will give me food? Where shall I go to sleep at night? Who will make me a new jacket? Oh, it would be better, a hundred times better, that I should die also! Yes, I want to die ... ih! ih! ih!"

And in his despair he tried to tear his hair; but his hair being made of wood, he could not even have the satisfaction of sticking his fingers into it.

Just then a large Pigeon flew over his head, and stopping with distended wings called down to him from a great height:

"Tell me, child, what are you doing there?"

"Don't you see? I am crying!" said Pinocchio, raising his head toward the voice and rubbing his eyes with his jacket.

"Tell me," continued the Pigeon, "among your companions, do you happen to know a puppet who is called Pinocchio?"

"Pinocchio? ... Did you say Pinocchio?" repeated the puppet, jumping quickly to his feet. "I am Pinocchio!"

The Pigeon at this answer descended rapidly to the ground. He was larger than a turkey.

"Do you also know Geppetto?" he asked.

"Do I know him! He is my poor papa! Has he perhaps spoken to you of me? Will you take me to him? Is he still alive? Answer me for pity's sake: is he still alive?"

"I left him three days ago on the seashore."

"What was he doing?"

"He was building a little boat for himself, to cross the ocean. For more than three months that poor man has been going all round the world looking for you. Not having succeeded in finding you, he has now taken it into his head to go to the distant countries of the new world in search of you."

"How far is it from here to the shore?" asked Pinocchio breathlessly.

"More than six hundred miles."

"Six hundred miles? Oh, beautiful Pigeon, what a fine thing it would be to have your wings! ..."

"If you wish to go, I will carry you there."

"How?"

"Astride on my back. Do you weigh much?"

"I weigh next to nothing. I am as light as a feather."

And without waiting for more, Pinocchio jumped at once on the Pigeon's back, and putting a leg on each

side of him as men do on horseback, he exclaimed joyfully:

"Gallop, gallop, my little horse, for I am anxious to arrive quickly!"

The Pigeon took flight, and in a few minutes had soared
so high that they almost touched the clouds. Finding himself at such an immense height the puppet had the curiosity to turn and look down; but his head spun round, and he
became so frightened that to save himself from the danger
of falling he would his arms tightly round the neck of his
feathered steed.

They flew all day. Toward evening the Pigeon said:

"I am very thirsty!"

"And I am very hungry!" rejoined Pinocchio.

"Let us stop at that dovecot for a few minutes, and then
we will continue our journey that we may reach the seashore by dawn tomorrow."

They went into a deserted dovecot, where they found
nothing but a basin full of water and a basket full of
vetch.

The puppet had never in his life been able to eat vetch:
according to him, it made him sick and revolted him. That
evening, however, he ate to repletion, and when he had
nearly emptied the basket he turned to the Pigeon and said
to him:

"I never could have believed that vetch was so
good!"

"Be assured, my boy," replied the Pigeon, "that when
hunger is real, and there is nothing else to eat, even vetch
becomes delicious. Hunger knows neither caprice nor
greediness."

Having quickly finished their little meal they recommenced their journey and flew away. The following morning they reached the seashore.

The Pigeon placed Pinocchio on the ground, and not
wishing to be troubled with thanks for having done a good
action, flew quickly away and disappeared.

The shore was crowded with people who were looking out to sea, shouting and gesticulating.

"What has happened?" asked Pinocchio of an old woman.

"A poor father who has lost his son has gone away in a boat to search for him on the other side of the water, and today the sea is tempestuous and the little boat is in danger of sinking."

"Where is the little boat?"

"It is out there in a line with my finger," said the old woman, pointing to a little boat which, seen at that distance, looked like a nutshell with a very little man in it.

Pinocchio fixed his eyes on it, and after looking attentively he gave a piercing scream, crying:

"It is my papa! It is my papa!"

The boat meanwhile, beaten by the fury of the waves, at one moment disappeared in the trough of the sea, and the next came again to the surface. Pinocchio, standing on the top of a high rock, kept calling to his father by name, and making every kind of signal to him with his hands, his handkerchief, and his cap.

And although he was so far off, Geppetto appeared to recognize his son, for he also took off his cap and waved it, and tried by gestures to make him understand that he would have returned if it had been possible, but that the sea was so tempestuous that he could not use his oars or approach the shore.

Suddenly a tremendous wave rose and the boat disappeared. They waited, hoping it would come again to the surface, but it was seen no more.

"Poor man!" said the fishermen who were assembled on the shore, and murmuring a prayer they turned to go home.

Just then they heard a desperate cry, and looking back they saw a little boy who exclaimed, as he jumped from a rock into the sea:

"I will save my papa!"

Pinocchio, being made of wood, floated easily and he swam like a fish. At one moment they saw him disappear under the water, carried down by the fury of the waves; and next he reappeared struggling with a leg or an arm. At last they lost sight of him and he was seen no more.

"Poor boy!" said the fishermen who were collected on the shore, and murmuring a prayer they returned home.

Chapter XXIV

PINOCCHIO *arrives at the* ISLAND OF THE INDUS-
TRIOUS BEES *and finds the* FAIRY *again*

Pinocchio, hoping to be in time to help his father, swam
the whole night.

And what a horrible night it was! The rain came down
in torrents, it hailed, the thunder was frightful, and the
flashes of lightning made it as light as day.

Toward morning he saw a long strip of land not far off.
It was an island in the midst of the sea.

He tried his utmost to reach the shore: but it was all in
vain. The waves, racing and tumbling over each other,
knocked him about as if he had been a stick or a wisp of
straw. At last, fortunately for him, a billow rolled up with
such fury and impetuosity that he was lifted up and thrown
violently far onto the sands.

He fell with such force that, as he struck the ground, his
ribs and all his joints cracked, but he comforted himself,
saying:

"This time also I have made a wonderful escape!"

Little by little the sky cleared, the sun shone out in all

his splendor, and the sea became as quiet and as smooth as oil.

The puppet put his clothes in the sun to dry, and began to look in every direction in hope of seeing on the vast expanse of water a little boat with a little man in it. But although he looked and looked, he could see nothing but the sky, and the sea, and the sail of some ship, but so far away that it seemed no bigger than a fly.

"If I only knew what this island was called!" he said to himself. "If I only knew whether it was inhabited by civilized people—I mean by people who haven't the bad habit of hanging boys to the branches of the trees. But who can I ask? Who, if there is nobody? . . ."

This idea of finding himself alone, alone, all alone, in the midst of this great uninhabited country, made him so melancholy that he was just beginning to cry. But at that moment, at a short distance from the shore, he saw a big fish swimming by; it was going quietly on its own business with its head out of the water.

Not knowing its name the puppet called to it in a loud voice to make himself heard:

"Eh, Sir Fish, will you permit me a word with you?"

"Two if you like," answered the fish, who was a Dolphin, and so polite that few like him are to be found in any sea in the world.

"Will you be kind enough to tell me if there are villages in this island where it would be possible to obtain something to eat, without running the danger of being eaten?"

"Certainly there are," replied the Dolphin. "Indeed, you will find one at a short distance from here."

"And what road must I take to go there?"

"You must take that path to your left and follow your nose. You cannot make a mistake."

"Will you tell me another thing? You who swim about the sea all day and all night, have you by chance met a little boat with my papa in it?"

"And who is your papa?"

"He is the best papa in the world, while it would be difficult to find a worse son than I am."

"During the terrible storm last night," answered the Dolphin, "the little boat must have gone to the bottom."

"And my papa?"

"He must have been swallowed by the terrible Dogfish who for some days past has been spreading devastation and ruin in our waters."

"Is this Dogfish very big?" asked Pinocchio, who was already beginning to quake with fear.

"Big! . . ." replied the Dolphin. "That you may form some idea of his size, I need only tell you that he is bigger than a five-storied house, and that his mouth is so enormous and so deep that a railway train with its smoking engine could pass easily down his throat."

"Mercy upon us!" exclaimed the terrified puppet; and putting on his clothes with the greatest haste he said to the Dolphin:

"Good-by, Sir Fish: excuse the trouble I have given you, and many thanks for your politeness."

He then took the path that had been pointed out to him and began to walk fast—so fast, indeed, that he was almost running. And at the slightest noise he turned to look behind him, fearing that he might see the terrible Dogfish with a railway train in its mouth following him.

After a walk of half an hour he reached a little village called the "Village of the Industrious Bees." The road was alive with people running here and there to attend to their business: all were at work, all had something to do. You could not have found an idler or a vagabond, not even if you had searched for him with a lighted lamp.

"Ah," said that lazy Pinocchio at once, "I see that this village will never suit me! I wasn't born to work!"

In the meanwhile he was tormented by hunger, for he had eaten nothing for twenty-four hours—not even vetch. What was he to do?

There were only two ways by which he could obtain

food—either by asking for a little work, or by begging for a halfpenny, or for a mouthful of bread.

He was ashamed to beg, for his father had always preached to him that no one had a right to beg except the aged and the infirm. The really poor in this world, deserving of compassion and assistance, are only those who from age or sickness are no longer able to earn their own bread with the labor of their hands. It is the duty of everyone else to work; and if they will not work, so much the worse for them if they suffer from hunger.

At that moment a man came down the road, tired and panting for breath. He was dragging along, with fatigue and difficulty, two carts full of charcoal.

Pinocchio, judging by his face that he was a kind man, approached him, and casting down his eyes with shame he said to him in a low voice:

"Would you have the charity to give me a half-penny, for I am dying of hunger?"

"You shall have not only a halfpenny," said the man, "but I will give you twopence, provided that you help me to drag home these two carts of charcoal."

"I am surprised at you!" answered the puppet in a tone of offense. "Let me tell you that I am not accustomed to do the work of a donkey: I have never drawn a cart!"

"So much the better for you," answered the man. "Then, my boy, if you are really dying of hunger, eat two fine slices of your pride, and be careful not to get indigestion."

A few minutes afterward a mason passed down the road carrying on his shoulders a basket of lime.

"Would you have the charity, good man, to give a half-penny to a poor boy who is yawning for want of food?"

"Willingly," answered the man. "Come with me and carry the lime, and instead of a halfpenny I will give you five."

"But the lime is heavy," objected Pinocchio, "and I don't want to tire myself."

"If you don't want to tire yourself, then, my boy, amuse yourself with yawning, and much good may it do you."

In less than half an hour twenty other people went by; and Pinocchio asked charity of them all, but they all answered:

"Are you not ashamed to beg? Instead of idling about the roads, go and look for a little work and learn to earn your bread."

At last a nice little woman carrying two cans of water came by.

"Will you let me drink a little water out of your can?" asked Pinocchio, who was burning with thirst.

"Drink, my boy, if you wish it!" said the little woman, setting down the two cans.

Pinocchio drank like a fish, and as he dried his mouth he mumbled:

"I have quenched my thirst. If I could only appease my hunger! . . ."

The good woman, hearing these words, said at once:

"If you will help me to carry home these two cans of water, I will give you a fine piece of bread."

Pinocchio looked at the can and answered neither yes nor no.

"And besides the bread you shall have a nice dish of cauliflower dressed with oil and vinegar," added the good woman.

Pinocchio gave another look at the can, and answered neither yes nor no.

"And after the cauliflower I will give you a beautiful bonbon full of syrup."

The temptation of this last dainty was so great that Pinocchio could resist no longer, and with an air of decision he said:

"I must have patience! I will carry the can to your house."

The can was heavy, and the puppet, not being strong enough to carry it in his hand, had to resign himself to carry it on his head.

When they reached the house the good little woman made Pinocchio sit down at a small table already laid and she placed before him the bread, the cauliflower, and the bonbon.

Pinocchio did not eat, he devoured. His stomach was like an apartment that had been left empty and uninhabited for five months.

When his ravenous hunger was somewhat appeased he raised his head to thank his benefactress; but he had no sooner looked at her than he gave a prolonged Oh-h-! of astonishment, and continued staring at her, with wide-open eyes, his fork in the air, and his mouth full of bread and cauliflower, as if he had been bewitched.

"What has surprised you so much?" asked the good woman, laughing.

"It is ..." answered the puppet, "it is ... it is ... that you are like ... that you remind me ... yes, yes, yes, the same voice ... the same eyes ... the same hair ... yes, yes, yes ... you also have blue hair ... as she had ... Oh, little Fairy! ... Tell me that it is you, really you! ... Do not make me cry any more! If you knew ... I have cried so much, I have suffered so much. ..."

And throwing himself at her feet on the floor, Pinocchio embraced the knees of the mysterious little woman and began to cry bitterly.

Chapter XXV

PINOCCHIO promises the FAIRY to be good and studious, for he is quite sick of being a puppet and wishes to become an exemplary boy

At first the good little woman maintained that she was not the little Fairy with blue hair; but seeing that she was found out, and not wishing to continue the comedy any longer, she ended by making herself known, and she said to Pinocchio:

"You little rogue! How did you ever discover who I was?"

"It was my great affection for you that told me."

"Do you remember? You left me a child, and now that you have found me again I am a woman—a woman almost old enough to be your mamma."

"I am delighted at that, for now, instead of calling you little sister, I will call you mamma. I have wished for such a long time to have a mamma like other boys! ... But how did you manage to grow so fast?"

"That is a secret."

"Teach it to me, for I should also like to grow. Don't you see? I always remain no bigger than a ninepin."

"But you cannot grow," replied the Fairy.

"Why?"

"Because puppets never grow. They are born puppets, live puppets, and die puppets."

"Oh, I am sick of being a puppet!" cried Pinocchio, giving himself a slap. "It is time that I became a man."

"And you will become one, if you know how to deserve it."

"Not really? And what can I do to deserve it?"

"A very easy thing: by learning to be a good boy."

"And you think I am not?"

"You are quite the contrary. Good boys are obedient, and you ..."

"And I never obey."

"Good boys like to learn and to work, and you ..."

"And I instead lead an idle vagabond life the year through."

"Good boys always speak the truth ..."

"And I always tell lies."

"Good boys go willingly to school ..."

"And school gives me pain all over my body. But from today I will change my life."

"Do you promise me?"

"I promise you. I will become a good little boy, and I will be the consolation of my papa. ... Where is my poor papa at this moment?"

"I do not know."

"Shall I ever have the happiness of seeing him again and kissing him?"

"I think so; indeed, I am sure of it."

At this answer Pinocchio was so delighted that he took the Fairy's hands and began to kiss them with such fervor that he seemed beside himself. Then raising his face and looking at her lovingly, he asked:

"Tell me, little mamma: then it was not true that you were dead?"

"It seems not," said the Fairy, smiling.

"If you only knew the sorrow I felt and the tightening of my throat when I read 'Here lies . . .' "

"I know it, and it is on that account that I have forgiven you. I saw from the sincerity of your grief that you had a good heart; and when boys have good hearts, even if they are scamps and have bad habits, there is always something to hope for: that is, there is always hope that they will turn to better ways. That is why I came to look for you here. I will be your mamma."

"Oh, how delightful!" shouted Pinocchio, jumping for joy.

"You must obey me and do everything that I bid you."

"Willingly, willingly, willingly!"

"Tomorrow," rejoined the Fairy, "you will begin to go to school."

Pinocchio became at once a little less joyful.

"Then you must choose an art, or a trade, according to your own wishes."

Pinocchio became very grave.

"What are you muttering between your teeth?" asked the Fairy in an angry voice.

"I was saying," moaned the puppet in a low voice, "that it seemed to me too late for me to go to school now. . . ."

"No, sir. Keep it in mind that it is never too late to learn and to instruct ourselves."

"But I do not wish to follow either an art or a trade."

"Why?"

"Because it tires me to work."

"My boy," said the Fairy, "those who talk in that way end almost always either in prison or in the hospital. Let me tell you that every man, whether he is born rich or poor, is obliged to do something in this world—to occupy himself, to work. Woe to those who lead slothful lives. Sloth is a dreadful illness and must be cured at once, in childhood. If not, when we are old it can never be cured."

Pinocchio was touched by these words, and lifting his head quickly he said to the Fairy:

"I will study, I will work, I will do all that you tell me, for indeed I have become weary of being a puppet, and I wish at any price to become a boy. You promised me that I should, did you not?"

"I did promise you, and it now depends upon yourself."

Chapter XXVI

PINOCCHIO accompanies his schoolfellows to the seashore to see the terrible DOGFISH

The following day Pinocchio went to the government school.

Imagine the delight of all the little rogues when they saw a puppet walk into their school! They set up a roar of laughter that never ended. They played all sorts of tricks on him. One boy carried off his cap, another pulled his jacket behind; one tried to give him a pair of inky mustachios just under his nose, and another attempted to tie strings to his feet and hands to make him dance.

For a short time Pinocchio pretended not to care and got on as well as he could; but at last, losing all patience, he turned to those who were teasing him most and making game of him, and said to them, looking very angry:

"Beware, boys: I am not come here to be your buffoon. I respect others, and I intend to be respected."

"Well said, boaster! You have spoken like a book!"

howled the young rascals, convulsed with mad laughter; and one of them, more impertinent than the others, stretched out his hand intending to seize the puppet by the end of his nose.

But he was not in time, for Pinocchio stuck his leg out from under the table and gave him a great kick on his shins.

"Oh, what hard feet!" roared the boy, rubbing the bruise that the puppet had given him.

"And what elbows! . . . Even harder than his feet!" said another, who for his rude tricks had received a blow in the stomach.

But nevertheless the kick and the blow acquired at once for Pinocchio the sympathy and the esteem of all the boys in the school. They all made friends with him and liked him heartily.

And even the master praised him, for he found him attentive, studious and intelligent—always the first to come to school, and the last to leave when school was over.

But he had one fault: he made too many friends; and among them were several young rascals well known for their dislike to study and love of mischief.

The master warned him every day, and even the good Fairy never failed to tell him, and to repeat constantly:

"Take care, Pinocchio! Those bad schoolfellows of yours will end sooner or later by making you lose all love of study, and perhaps even they may bring upon you some great misfortune."

"There is no fear of that!" answered the puppet, shrugging his shoulders and touching his forehead as much as to say: "There is so much sense here!"

Now it happened that one fine day, as he was on his way to school, he met several of his usual companions who, coming up to him, asked:

"Have you heard the great news?"

"No."

"In the sea near here a Dogfish has appeared as big as a mountain."

"Not really? Can it be the same Dogfish that was there when my poor papa was drowned?"

"We are going to the shore to see him. Will you come with us?"

"No; I am going to school."

"What matters school? We can go to school tomorrow. Whether we have a lesson more or a lesson less, we shall always remain the same donkeys."

"But what will the master say?"

"The master may say what he likes. He is paid on purpose to grumble all day."

"And my mamma?"

"Mammas know nothing," answered those bad little boys.

"Do you know what I will do?" said Pinocchio. "I have reasons for wishing to see the Dogfish, but I will go and see him when school is over."

"Poor donkey!" exclaimed one of the number. "Do you suppose that a fish of that size will wait your convenience? As soon as he is tired of being here he will start for another place, and then it will be too late."

"How long does it take from here to the shore?" asked the puppet.

"We can be there and back in an hour."

"Then away!" shouted Pinocchio. "And he who runs fastest is the best!"

Having thus given the signal to start, the boys, with their books and copybooks under their arms, rushed off across the fields, and Pinocchio was always the first—he seemed to have wings to his feet.

From time to time he turned to jeer at his companions, who were some distance behind, and seeing them panting for breath, covered with dust and their tongues hanging out of their mouths, he laughed heartily. The unfortunate boy little knew what terrors and horrible disasters he was going to meet with!

Chapter XXVII

Great fight between PINOCCHIO *and his companions. One of them is wounded, and* PINOCCHIO *is arrested by the gendarmes*

When he arrived on the shore Pinocchio looked out to sea; but he saw no Dogfish. The sea was as smooth as a great crystal mirror.

"Where is the Dogfish?" he asked, turning to his companions.

"He must have gone to have his breakfast," said one of them, laughing.

"Or he has thrown himself on to his bed to have a little nap," added another, laughing still louder.

From their absurd answers and silly laughter Pinocchio perceived that his companions had been making a fool of him, in inducing him to believe a tale with no truth in it. Taking it very badly, he said to them angrily:

"And now may I ask what fun you could find in deceiving me with the story of the Dogfish?"

"Oh, it was great fun!" answered the little rascals in chorus.

"And in what did it consist?"

"In making you miss school, and persuading you to come with us. Are you not ashamed of being always so punctual and so diligent with your lessons? Are you not ashamed of studying so hard?"

"And if I study hard what concern is it of yours?"

"It concerns us excessively, because it makes us appear in a bad light to the master."

"Why?"

"Because boys who study make those who, like us, have no wish to learn seem worse by comparison. And that is too bad. We too have our pride!"

"Then what must I do to please you?"

"You must follow our example and hate school, lessons, and the master—our three greatest enemies."

"And if I wish to continue my studies?"

"In that case we will have nothing more to do with you, and at the first opportunity we will make you pay for it."

"Really," said the puppet, shaking his head, "you make me inclined to laugh."

"Eh, Pinocchio!" shouted the biggest of the boys, confronting him. "None of your superior airs; don't come here to crow over us! ... For if you are not afraid of us, we are not afraid of you. Remember that you are one against seven of us."

"Seven, like the seven deadly sins," said Pinocchio, with a shout of laughter.

"Listen to him! He has insulted us all! He called us the seven deadly sins!"

"Pinocchio! Beg pardon ... or it will be the worse for you!"

"Cuckoo!" sang the puppet, putting his forefinger to the end of his nose·scoffingly.

"Pinocchio! It will end badly!"

"Cuckoo!"

"You will get as many blows as a donkey!"

"Cuckoo!"

"You will return home with a broken nose!"

"Cuckoo!"

"Ah, you shall have the cuckoo from me!" said the most courageous of the boys. "Take that to begin with, and keep it for your supper tonight."

And so saying he gave him a blow on the head with his fist.

But it was give-and-take; for the puppet, as was to be expected, immediately returned the blow, and the fight in a moment became general and desperate.

Pinocchio, although he was one alone, defended himself like a hero. He used his feet, which were of the hardest wood, to such purpose that he kept his enemies at a respectful distance. Wherever they touched they left a bruise by way of reminder.

The boys, becoming furious at not being able to measure themselves hand to hand with the puppet, had recourse to other weapons. Loosening their satchels they commenced throwing their schoolbooks at him—grammars, dictionaries, spelling books, geography books, and other scholastic works. But Pinocchio was quick and had sharp eyes, and always managed to duck in time, so that the books passed over his head and all fell into the sea.

Imagine the astonishment of the fish! Thinking that the books were something to eat, they all arrived in shoals, but having tasted a page or two, or a frontispiece, they spat it quickly out and made a wry face that seemed to say: "It isn't food for us; we are accustomed to something much better!"

The battle meantime had become fiercer than ever, when a big Crab, who had come out of the water and had climbed slowly up on the shore, called out in a hoarse voice that sounded like a trumpet with a bad cold:

"Have done with that, you young ruffians, for you are nothing else! These hand-to-hand fights between boys seldom finish well. Some disaster is sure to happen!"

Poor Crab! He might as well have preached to the wind. Even that young rascal Pinocchio, turning around, looked at him mockingly and said rudely:

"Hold your tongue, you tiresome Crab! You had better suck some licorice lozenges to cure that cold in your throat. Or better still, go to bed and try to get a reaction!"

Just then the boys, who had no more books of their own to throw, spied at a little distance the satchel that belonged to Pinocchio, and took possession of it in less time than it takes to tell.

Among the books there was one bound in strong cardboard with the back and points of parchment. It was a Treatise on Arithmetic. I leave you to imagine if it was big or not!

One of the boys seized this volume, and aiming at Pinocchio's head threw it at him with all the force he could muster. But instead of hitting the puppet it struck one of his companions on the temple, who, turning as white as a sheet, said only:

"Oh, Mother, help! . . . I am dying!" and fell his whole length on the sand. Thinking he was dead, the terrified boys ran off as hard as their legs could carry them, and in a few minutes they were out of sight.

But Pinocchio remained. Although from grief and fright he was more dead than alive, nevertheless, he ran and soaked his handkerchief in the sea and began to bathe the temples of his poor schoolfellow. Crying bitterly in his despair he kept calling him by name and saying to him:

"Eugene! . . . My poor Eugene! . . . Open your eyes and look at me! . . . Why do you not answer? I did not do it, indeed it was not I that hurt you so! Believe me, it was not! Open your eyes, Eugene. . . . If you keep your eyes shut I shall die too. . . . Oh! What shall I do? How shall I ever return home? How can I ever have the courage to go

back to my good mamma? What will become of me? ...
Where can I fly to? ... Oh, how much better it would
have been, a thousand times better, if I had only gone to
school! ... Why did I listen to my companions? They
have been my ruin. The master said to me, and my
mamma repeated it often: 'Beware of bad companions!'
But I am obstinate ... a willful fool.... I let them talk
and then I always take my own way! And I have to suffer
for it.... And so, ever since I have been in the world, I
have never had a happy quarter of an hour. Oh, dear, what
will become of me, what will become of me, what will become of me? ..."

And Pinocchio began to cry and sob, and to strike
his head with his fists, and to call poor Eugene by his
name. Suddenly he heard the sound of approaching footsteps.

He turned and saw two carabineers.

"What are you doing there lying on the ground?" they
asked Pinocchio.

"I am helping my schoolfellow."

"Has he been hurt?"

"So it seems."

"Hurt indeed!" said one of the carabineers, stooping
down and examining Eugene closely.

"This boy has been wounded in the temple. Who
wounded him?"

"Not I," stammered the puppet breathlessly.

"If it was not you, then who was it?"

"Not I," repeated Pinocchio.

"And with what was he wounded?"

"With this book." And the puppet picked up from the
ground the Treatise on Arithmetic, bound in cardboard and
parchment, and showed it to the carabineer.

"And to whom does this belong?"

"To me."

"That is enough; nothing more is wanted. Get up and
come with us at once."

"But I am innocent!"

"Come along with us!"

"But I am innocent."

"Come along with us!"

Before they left, the carabineers called some fishermen, who were passing at that moment near the shore in their boat, and said to them:

"We give this boy who has been wounded in the head into your charge. Carry him to your house and nurse him. Tomorrow we will come and see him."

They then turned to Pinocchio, and having placed him between them they said to him in a commanding voice:

"Forward! And walk quickly, or it will be the worse for you."

Without requiring it to be repeated, the puppet set out along the road leading to the village. But the poor little devil hardly knew where he was. He thought he must be dreaming, and what a dreadful dream! He was beside himself. He saw double; his legs shook; his tongue clung to the roof of his mouth, and he could not utter a word. And yet in the midst of his stupefaction and apathy his heart was pierced by a cruel thorn—the thought that he would have to pass under the windows of the good Fairy's house between the carabineers. He would rather have died.

They had already reached the village when a gust of wind blew Pinocchio's cap off his head and carried it ten yards off.

"Will you permit me," said the puppet to the carabineers, "to go and get my cap?"

"Go, then; but be quick about it."

The puppet went and picked up his cap ... but instead of putting it on his head he took it between his teeth and began to run as hard as he could toward the seashore.

The carabineers, thinking it would be difficult to overtake him, sent after him a large mastiff who had won the first prize at all the dog races. Pinocchio ran,

but the dog ran faster. The people came to their windows
and crowded into the street in their anxiety to see the end
of the desperate race. But they could not satisfy their curiosity, for Pinocchio and the dog raised such clouds of
dust that in a few minutes nothing could be seen of either
of them.

Chapter XXVIII

PINOCCHIO *is in danger of being fried in a frying pan like a fish*

There came a moment in this desperate race—a terrible moment when Pinocchio thought himself lost: for you must know that Alidoro—for so the mastiff was called—had run so swiftly that he had nearly caught up with him.

The puppet could hear the panting of the dreadful beast close behind him; there was not a hand's breath between them; he could even feel the dog's hot breath.

Fortunately the shore was close and the sea but a few steps off.

As soon as he reached the sands the puppet made a wonderful leap—a frog could have done no better—and plunged into the water.

Alidoro, on the contrary, wished to stop himself; but carried away by the impetus of the race he also went into the sea. The unfortunate dog could not swim, but he made great efforts to keep himself afloat with his paws; but the more he struggled the farther he sank head downward under the water.

When he rose to the surface again his eyes were rolling with terror, and he barked out:

"I am drowning! I am drowning!"

"Drown!" shouted Pinocchio from a distance, seeing himself safe from all danger.

"Help me, dear Pinocchio! . . . Save me from death!"

At that agonizing cry the puppet, who had in reality an excellent heart, was moved with compassion, and turning to the dog he said:

"But if I save your life, will you promise to give me no further annoyance, and not to run after me?"

"I promise! I promise! Be quick, for pity's sake, for if you delay another half minute I shall be dead."

Pinocchio hesitated; but remembering that his father had often told him that a good action is never lost, he swam to Alidoro, and taking hold of his tail with both hands brought him safe and sound on to the dry sand of the beach.

The poor dog could not stand. He had drunk, against his will, so much salt water that he was like a balloon. The puppet, however, not wishing to trust him too far, thought it more prudent to jump again into the water. When he had swum some distance from the shore he called out to the friend he had rescued:

"Good-by, Alidoro; a good journey to you, and take my compliments to all at home."

"Good-by, Pinocchio," answered the dog. "A thousand thanks for having saved my life. You have done me a great service, and in this world what is given is returned. If an occasion offers I shall not forget it."

Pinocchio swam on, keeping always near the land. At last he thought that he had reached a safe place. Giving a look along the shore, he saw among the rocks a kind of cave from which a cloud of smoke was ascending.

"In that cave," he said to himself, "there must be a fire. So much the better. I will go and dry and warm myself, and then? . . . And then we shall see."

Having taken the resolution, he approached the rocks;

but as he was going to climb up, he felt something under the water that rose higher and higher and carried him into the air. He tried to escape, but it was too late, for to his extreme surprise he found himself enclosed in a great net, together with a swarm of fish of every size and shape, who were flapping and struggling like so many despairing souls.

At the same moment a fisherman came out of the cave; he was so ugly, so horribly ugly, that he looked like a sea monster. Instead of hair his head was covered with a thick bush of green grass, his skin was green, his eyes were green, his long beard that came down to the ground was also green. He had the appearance of an immense lizard standing on its hind paws.

When the fisherman had drawn his net out of the sea, he exclaimed with great satisfaction:

"Thank Heaven! Again today I shall have a splendid feast of fish!"

"What a mercy that I am not a fish!" said Pinocchio to himself, regaining a little courage.

The net full of fish was carried into the cave, which was dark and smoky. In the middle of the cave a large frying pan full of oil was frying, and sending out a smell of mushrooms that was suffocating.

"Now we will see what fish we have taken!" said the green fisherman; and putting into the net an enormous hand, so out of all proportion that it looked like a baker's shovel, he pulled out a handful of mullet.

"These mullet are good!" he said, looking at them and smelling them complacently. And after he had smelt them he threw them into a pan without water.

He repeated the same operation many times; and as he drew out the fish, his mouth watered and he said, chuckling to himself:

"What good whiting! ...

"What exquisite sardines! ...

"These soles are delicious! ...

"And these crabs excellent! ...

"What dear little anchovies! . . ."

I need not tell you that the whiting, the sardines, the soles, the crabs, and the anchovies were all thrown promiscuously into the pan to keep company with the mullet.

The last to remain in the net was Pinocchio.

No sooner had the fisherman taken him out than he opened his big green eyes with astonishment, and cried, half frightened:

"What species of fish is this? I never remember eating this kind of fish!"

And he looked at him again attentively, and having examined him well all over, he ended by saying:

"I know: he must be a crawfish."

Pinocchio, mortified at being mistaken for a crawfish, said in an angry voice:

"A crawfish indeed! Do you take me for a crawfish? What treatment! Let me tell you that I am a puppet."

"A puppet?" replied the fisherman. "To tell the truth, a puppet is quite a new fish for me. All the better! I shall eat you with greater pleasure."

"Eat me! But will you understand that I am not a fish? Do you not hear that I talk and reason as you do?"

"That is quite true," said the fisherman. "And as I see that you are a fish possessed of the talent of talking and reasoning as I do, I will treat you with all the attention that is your due."

"And this attention? . . ."

"In token of my friendship and particular regard, I will leave you the choice of how you would like to be cooked. Would you like to be fried in the frying pan, or would you prefer to be stewed with tomato sauce?"

"To tell the truth," answered Pinocchio, "if I am to choose, I should prefer to be set at liberty and to return home."

"You are joking! Do you imagine that I would lose the opportunity of tasting such a rare fish? It is not every day, I assure you, that a puppet fish is caught in these waters. Leave it to me. I will fry you in the frying pan with the other fish, and you will be quite satisfied. It is always consolation to be fried in company."

At this speech the unhappy Pinocchio began to cry and scream and to implore for mercy; and he said, sobbing: "How much better it would have been if I had gone to school! . . . I would listen to my companions and now I am paying for it! Ih! . . . Ih! . . . Ih! . . ."

And he wriggled like an eel, and made indescribable efforts to slip out of the clutches of the green fisherman. But it was useless; the fisherman took a long strip of rush, and having bound his hands and feet as if he had been a sausage, he threw him into the pan with the other fish.

He then fetched a wooden bowl full of flour and began to flour them each in turn, and as soon as they were ready he threw them into the frying pan.

The first to dance in the boiling oil were the poor whiting; the crabs followed, then the sardines, then the soles, then the anchovies, and at last it was Pinocchio's turn. Seeing himself so near death, and such a horrible death, he was so frightened, and trembled so violently, that he had neither voice nor breath left for further entreaties.

But the poor boy implored with his eyes! The green fisherman, however, without caring in the least, plunged him five or six times in the flour, until he was white from head to foot, and looked like a puppet made of plaster.

He then took him by the head, and . . .

Chapter XXIX

He returns to the FAIRY'S *house. She promises him that the following day he shall cease to be a puppet and shall become a boy. Grand breakfast of coffee and milk to celebrate this great event*

Just as the fisherman was on the point of throwing Pinocchio into the frying pan a large dog entered the cave, enticed there by the strong and savory odor of fried fish.

"Get out!" shouted the fisherman threateningly, holding the floured puppet in his hand.

But the poor dog, who was as hungry as a wolf, whined and wagged his tail as much as to say:

"Give me a mouthful of fish and I will leave you in peace."

"Get out, I tell you!" repeated the fisherman, and he stretched out his leg to give him a kick.

But the dog, who, when he was really hungry, would not stand trifling, turned upon him, growling and showing his terrible tusks.

At that moment a little feeble voice was heard in the cave saying entreatingly:

"Save me, Alidoro! If you do not save me I shall be fried!"

The dog recognized Pinocchio's voice, and to his extreme surprise perceived that it proceeded from the floured bundle that the fisherman held in his hand.

So what do you think he did? He made a spring, seized the bundle in his mouth, and holding it gently between his teeth he rushed out of the cave and was gone like a flash of lightning.

The fisherman, furious at seeing a fish he was so anxious to eat snatched from him, ran after the dog; but he had not gone many steps when he was taken with a fit of coughing and had to give up the chase.

Alidoro, when he had reached the path that led to the village, stopped, and put his friend Pinocchio gently on to the ground.

"How much I have to thank you for!" said the puppet.

"There is no necessity," replied the dog. "You saved me and I have now returned it. You know that we must all help each other in this world."

"But how did you happen to come to the cave?"

"I was lying on the shore more dead than alive when the wind brought to me the smell of fried fish. The smell excited my appetite, and I followed it up. If I had arrived a second later . . ."

"Do not mention it!" groaned Pinocchio, who was still trembling with fright. "Do not mention it! If you had arrived a second later I should by this time have been fried, eaten, and digested. Brrr! . . . It makes me shudder only to think of it!"

Alidoro, laughing, extended his right paw to the puppet, who shook it heartily in token of great friendship, and they then separated.

The dog took the road home; and Pinocchio, left alone, went to a cottage not far off, and said to a little old man who was warming himself in the sun:

"Tell me, good man, do you know anything of a poor boy called Eugene who was wounded in the head?"

"The boy was brought by some fishermen to this cottage, and now . . ."

"And now he is dead!" interrupted Pinocchio with great sorrow.

"No, he is alive, and has returned to his home."

"Not really? Not really?" cried the puppet, dancing with delight. "Then the wound was not serious?"

"It might have been very serious and even fatal," answered the little old man, "for they threw a thick book bound in cardboard at his head."

"And who threw it at him?"

"One of his schoolfellows, a certain Pinocchio."

"And who is this Pinocchio?" asked the puppet, pretending ignorance.

"They say that he is a bad boy, a vagabond, a regular good-for-nothing."

"Calumnies! All calumnies!"

"Do you know this Pinocchio?"

"By sight!" answered the puppet.

"And what is your opinion of him?" asked the little man.

"He seems to me to be a very good boy, anxious to learn, and obedient and affectionate to his father and family."

While the puppet was firing off all these lies, he touched his nose and perceived that it had lengthened more than a hand. Very much alarmed, he began to cry out:

"Don't believe, good man, what I have been telling you. I know Pinocchio very well, and I can assure you that he is really a very bad boy, disobedient and idle, who instead of going to school runs off with his companions to amuse himself."

He had hardly finished speaking when his nose became shorter and returned to the same size that it was before.

"And why are you all covered with white?" asked the old man suddenly.

"I will tell you. . . . Without observing it, I rubbed myself against a wall which had been freshly whitewashed," answered the puppet, ashamed to confess that he had been floured like a fish prepared for the frying pan.

"And what have you done with your jacket, your trousers, and your cap?"

"I met with robbers who took them from me. Tell me, good old man, could you perhaps give me some clothes to return home in?"

"My boy, as to clothes, I have nothing but a little sack in which I keep beans. If you wish it, take it; there it is."

Pinocchio did not wait to be told twice. He took the sack at once, and with a pair of scissors he cut a hole at the end and at side, and put it on like a shirt. And with this slight clothing he set off for the village.

But as he went he did not feel at all comfortable—so little so, indeed, that for a step forward he took another backwards, and he said, talking to himself:

"How shall I ever present myself to my good little Fairy? What will she say when she sees me? Will she forgive me this second escapade? I bet that she will not forgive me! Oh, I am sure that she will not forgive me! . . . And it serves me right, for I am a rascal. I am always promising to correct myself, and I never keep my word!"

When he reached the village it was night and very dark. A storm had come on, and as the rain was coming down in torrents he went straight to the Fairy's house, resolved to knock at the door, and hoping to be let in.

But when he was there his courage failed him, and instead of knocking he ran away some twenty paces. He returned to the door a second time, but could not make up his mind; he came back a third time, still he dared not; the fourth time he laid hold of the knocker and, trembling, gave a little knock.

He waited and waited. At last, after half an hour had passed, a window on the top floor was opened—the house was four stories high—and Pinocchio saw a big Snail with a lighted candle on her head looking out. She called to him:

"Who is there at this hour?"

"Is the Fairy at home?" asked the puppet.

"The Fairy is asleep and must not be awakened; but who are you?"

"It is I!"

"Who is I?"

"Pinocchio."

"And who is Pinocchio?"

"The puppet who lives in the Fairy's house."

"Ah, I understand!" said the Snail. "Wait for me there. I will come down and open the door directly."

"Be quick, for pity's sake, for I am dying of cold."

"My boy, I am a snail, and snails are never in a hurry."

An hour passed, and then two, and the door was not opened. Pinocchio, who was wet through, and trembling from cold and fear, at last took courage and knocked again, and this time he knocked louder.

At this second knock a window on the lower story opened, and the same Snail appeared at it.

"Beautiful little Snail," cried Pinocchio from the street, "I have been waiting for two hours! And two hours on such a bad night seem longer than two years. Be quick, for pity's sake."

"My boy," answered the calm, phlegmatic little animal—"my boy, I am a snail, and snails are never in a hurry."

And the window was shut again.

Shortly afterward midnight struck; then one o'clock, then two o'clock, and the door remained still closed.

Pinocchio at last, losing all patience, seized the knocker in a rage, intending to give a blow that would resound through the house. But the knocker, which was iron, turned suddenly into an eel, and slipping out of his hands disappeared in the stream of water that ran down the middle of the street.

"Ah! Is that it?" shouted Pinocchio, blind with rage. "Since the knocker has disappeared, I will kick instead with all my might."

And drawing a little back he gave a tremendous kick against the house door. The blow was indeed so violent that his foot went through the wood and stuck; and when he tried to draw it back again it was trouble thrown away, for it remained fixed like a nail that has been hammered down.

Think of poor Pinocchio! He was obliged to spend the remainder of the night with one foot on the ground and the other in the air.

The following morning at daybreak the door was at last opened. That clever little Snail had taken only nine hours to come down from the fourth story to the house door. It is evident that her exertions must have been great.

"What are you doing with your foot stuck in the door?" she asked the puppet, laughing.

"It was an accident. Do try, beautiful Snail, and see if you cannot release me from this torture."

"My boy, that is the work of a carpenter, and I have never been a carpenter."

"Beg the Fairy for me!"

"The Fairy is asleep and must not be awakened."

"But what do you suppose that I can do all day nailed to this door?"

"Amuse yourself by counting the ants that pass down the street."

"Bring me at least something to eat, for I am quite exhausted."

"At once," said the Snail.

In fact, after three hours and a half she returned to Pinocchio carrying a silver tray on her head. The tray contained a loaf of bread, a roast chicken, and four ripe apricots.

"Here is the breakfast that the Fairy has sent you," said the Snail.

The puppet felt very much comforted at the sight of these good things. But when he began to eat them, what was his dismay at making the discovery that the bread was plaster, the chicken cardboard, and the four apricots painted alabaster.

He wanted to cry. In his desperation he tried to throw away the tray and all that was on it; but instead, either from grief or exhaustion, he fainted away.

When he came to himself he found that he was lying on a sofa, and the Fairy was beside him.

"I will pardon you once more," the Fairy said, "but woe to you if you behave badly a third time!"

Pinocchio promised and swore that he would study, and that for the future he would always conduct himself well.

And he kept his word for the remainder of the year. Indeed, at the examinations before the holidays, he had the honor of being the first in the school, and his behavior in general was so satisfactory and praiseworthy that the Fairy was very much pleased, and said to him:

"Tomorrow your wish shall be gratified."

"And that is?"

"Tomorrow you shall cease to be a wooden puppet, and you shall become a boy."

No one who had not witnessed it could ever imagine Pinocchio's joy at this long-sighed-for good fortune. All his schoolfellows were to be invited for the following day to a grand breakfast at the Fairy's house, that they might celebrate together the great event. The Fairy had prepared two hundred cups of coffee and milk, and four hundred rolls cut and buttered on each side. The day promised to be most happy and delightful, but . . .

Unfortunately, in the lives of puppets there is always a "but" that spoils everything.

Chapter XXX

PINOCCHIO, *instead of becoming a boy, starts se-cretly with his friend* CANDLEWICK *for the* LAND OF BOOBIES

Pinocchio, as was natural, asked the Fairy's permission to go round the town to make the invitations; and the Fairy said to him:

"Go if you like and invite your companions for the breakfast tomorrow, but remember to return home before dark. Have you understood?"

"I promise to be back in an hour," answered the puppet.

"Take care, Pinocchio! Boys are always very ready to promise; but generally they are little given to keep their word."

"But I am not like other boys. When I say a thing, I do it."

"We shall see. If you are disobedient, so much the worse for you."

"Why?"

"Because boys who do not listen to the advice of those who know more than they do always meet with some misfortune or other."

"I have experienced that," said Pinocchio. "But I shall never make that mistake again."

"We shall see if that is true."

Without saying more the puppet took leave of his good Fairy, who was like a mamma to him, and went out of the house singing and dancing.

In less than an hour all his friends were invited. Some accepted at once heartily; others at first required pressing; but when they heard that the rolls to be eaten with the coffee were to be buttered on both sides, they ended by saying:

"We will come also, to do you a pleasure."

Now I must tell you that among Pinocchio's friends and schoolfellows there was one that he greatly preferred and was very fond of. This boy's name was Romeo; but he always went by the nickname of Candlewick, because he was so thin, straight, and bright like the new wick of a little night light.

Candlewick was the laziest and the naughtiest boy in the school; but Pinocchio was devoted to him. He had indeed gone at once to his house to invite him to the breakfast, but he had not found him. He returned a second time, but Candlewick was not there. He went a third time, but it was in vain. Where could he search for him? He looked here, there, and everywhere, and at last he saw him hiding in the porch of a peasant's cottage.

"What are you doing there?" asked Pinocchio, coming up to him.

"I am waiting for midnight, to start . . ."

"Why, where are you going?"

"Very far, very far, very far away."

"And I have been three times to your house to look for you."

"What did you want with me?"

"Do you not know the great event? Have you not heard of my good fortune?"

"What is it?"

"Tomorrow I cease to be a puppet, and I become a boy like you, and like all the other boys."

"Much good may it do you."

"Tomorrow, therefore, I expect you to breakfast at my house."

"But when I tell you that I am going away tonight ..."

"At what o'clock?"

"In a short time."

"And where are you going?"

"I am going to live in a country ... the most delightful country in the world: a real land of Cocagne!"

"And how is it called?"

"It is called the 'Land of Boobies.' Why do you not come too?"

"I? No, never!"

"You are wrong, Pinocchio. Believe me, if you do not come you will repent it. Where could you find a better country for us boys? There are no schools there; there are no masters; there are no books. In that delightful land nobody ever studies. On Thursday there is never school; and every week consists of six Thursdays and one Sunday. Only think, the autumn holidays begin on the first of January and finish on the last day of December. That is the country for me! That is what all civilized countries should be like!"

"But how are the days spent in the Land of Boobies?"

"They are spent in play and amusement from morning till night. When night comes you go to bed, and recommence the same life in the morning. What do you think of it?"

"Hum! ..." said Pinocchio; and he shook his head slightly as much as to say, "That is a life that I also would willingly lead."

"Well, will you go with me? Yes or no? Resolve quickly."

"No, no, no, and again no. I promised my good Fairy to become a well-conducted boy, and I will keep my word. And as I see that the sun is setting I must leave you at once and run away. Good-by, and a pleasant journey to you."

"Where are you rushing off to in such a hurry?"

"Home. My good Fairy wishes me to be back before dark."

"Wait another two minutes."

"It will make me too late."

"Only two minutes."

"And if the Fairy scolds me?"

"Let her scold. When she has scolded well, she will hold her tongue," said that rascal Candlewick.

"And what are you going to do? Are you going alone or with companions?"

"Alone? We will be more than a hundred boys."

"And do you make the journey on foot?"

"A coach will pass by shortly which is to take me to that happy country."

"What would I not give for the coach to pass by now!"

"Why?"

"That I might see you all start together."

"Stay here a little longer and you will see us."

"No, no, I must go home."

"Wait another two minutes."

"I have already delayed too long. The Fairy will be anxious about me."

"Poor Fairy! Is she afraid that the bats will eat you?"

"But now," continued Pinocchio, "are you really certain that there are no schools in that country?"

"Not even the shadow of one."

"And no masters either?"

"Not one."

"And no one is ever made to study?"

"Never, never, never!"

"What a delightful country!" said Pinocchio, his mouth watering. "What a delightful country! I have never been there, but I can quite imagine it . . ."

"Why will you not come also?"

"It is useless to tempt me. I promised my good Fairy to become a sensible boy, and I will not break my word."

"Good-by, then, and give my compliments to all the boys at the gymnasiums, and also to those of the lyceums, if you meet them in the street."

"Good-by, Candlewick. A pleasant journey to you, amuse yourself, and think sometimes of your friends."

Thus saying the puppet made two steps to go, but then stopped, and turning to his friend he inquired:

"But are you quite certain that in that country all the weeks consist of six Thursdays and one Sunday?"

"Most certain."

"But do you know for certain that the holidays begin on the first of January and finish on the last day of December?"

"Assuredly."

"What a delightful country!" repeated Pinocchio, looking enchanted. Then, with a resolute air, he added in a great hurry:

"This time really good-by, and a pleasant journey to you."

"Good-by."

"When do you start?"

"Shortly."

"What a pity! If really it wanted only an hour to the time of your start, I should be almost tempted to wait."

"And the Fairy?"

"It is already late . . . If I return home an hour sooner or an hour later it will be all the same."

"Poor Pinocchio! And if the Fairy scolds you?"

"I must have patience! I will let her scold. When she has scolded well, she will hold her tongue."

In the meantime night had come on and it was quite dark. Suddenly they saw in the distance a small light moving . . . and they heard a noise of talking, and the sound of a trumpet, but so small and feeble that it resembled the hum of a mosquito.

"Here it is!" shouted Candlewick, jumping to his feet.

"What is it?" asked Pinocchio in a whisper.

"It is the coach coming to take me. Now will you come, yes or no?"

"But is it really true," asked the puppet, "that in that country boys are never obliged to study?"

"Never, never, never!"

"What a delightful country! . . . What a delightful country! . . . What a delightful country!"

Chapter XXXI

After five months' residence in the land of CO-CAGNE, PINOCCHIO, *to his great astonishment, grows a beautiful pair of donkey's ears, and he becomes a little donkey, tail and all*

At last the coach arrived; and it arrived without making the slightest noise, for its wheels were bound round with tow and rags.

It was drawn by twelve pairs of donkeys, all the same size but of different colors.

Some were gray, some white, some brindled like pepper and salt, and others had large stripes of yellow and blue.

But the most extraordinary thing was this: the twelve pairs, that is, the twenty-four donkeys, instead of being shod like other beasts of burden, had on their feet men's boots made of white kid.

And the coachman? . . .

Picture to yourself a little man broader than he was long, flabby and greasy like a lump of butter, with a small round face like an orange, a little mouth that was always laughing, and a soft caressing voice like a cat when she is trying to insinuate herself into the good graces of the mistress of the house.

All the boys as soon as they saw him fell in love with

him, and vied with each other in taking places in his coach
to be conducted to the true land of Cocagne, known on the
geographical map by the seducing name of the Land of
Boobies.

The coach was in fact quite full of boys between eight
and twelve years old, heaped one upon another like her-
rings in a barrel. They were uncomfortable, packed close
together, and could hardly breathe: but nobody said Oh!—
nobody grumbled. The consolation of knowing that in a
few hours they would reach a country where there were no
books, no schools, and no masters made them so happy
and resigned that they felt neither fatigue nor inconve-
nience, neither hunger, nor thirst, nor want of sleep.

As soon as the coach had drawn up, the little man
turned to Candlewick, and with a thousand smirks and grimaces said to him, smiling:

"Tell me, my fine boy, would you also like to go to that
fortunate country?"

"I certainly wish to go."

"But I must warn you, my dear child, that there is not
a place left in the coach. You can see for yourself that it
is quite full."

"No matter," replied Candlewick. "If there is no place
inside, I will manage to sit on the springs."

And giving a leap he seated himself astride of the
springs.

"And you, my love," said the little man, turning in a
flattering manner to Pinocchio, "what do you intend to do?
Are you coming with us, or are you going to remain behind?"

"I remain behind," answered Pinocchio. "I am going
home. I intend to study and to earn a good character at
school, as all well-conducted boys do."

"Much good may it do you!"

"Pinocchio!" called out Candlewick. "Listen to me:
come with us and we shall have such fun."

"No, no, no!"

"Come with us, and we shall have such fun," cried four other voices from the inside of the coach.

"Come with us, and we shall have such fun," shouted in chorus, a hundred voices from the inside of the coach.

"But if I come with you, what will my good Fairy say?" said the puppet, who was beginning to yield.

"Do not trouble your head with melancholy thoughts. Consider only that we are going to a country where we shall be at liberty to run riot from morning till night."

Pinocchio did not answer; but he sighed; he sighed again; he sighed for the third time, and he said finally:

"Make a little room for me, for I am coming too."

"The places are all full," replied the little man, "but to show you how welcome you are, you shall have my seat on the box."

"And you?"

"Oh, I will go on foot."

"No, indeed, I could not allow that. I would rather mount one of these donkeys," cried Pinocchio.

Approaching the right-hand donkey of the first pair he attempted to mount him, but the animal turned on him, and giving him a great blow in the stomach rolled him over with his legs in the air.

You can imagine the impertinent and immoderate laughter of all the boys who witnessed this scene.

But the little man did not laugh. He approached the rebellious donkey and, pretending to give him a kiss, bit off half of his ear.

Pinocchio in the meantime had got up from the ground in a fury, and with a spring he seated himself on the poor animal's back. And he sprang so well that the boys stopped laughing and began to shout: "Hurrah, Pinocchio!" And they clapped their hands and applauded him as if they would never finish.

But the donkey suddenly kicked up its hind legs, and backing violently threw the poor puppet into the middle of the road onto a heap of stones.

The roars of laughter recommenced; but the little man,

instead of laughing, felt such affection for the restive ass that he kissed him again, and as he did so he bit half of his other ear clean off. He then said to the puppet:

"Mount him now without fear. That little donkey had got some whim into his head; but I whispered something in his ear, and I think he'll be obedient and gentle now."

Pinocchio mounted again, and the coach started to move; but while the donkeys galloped and the coach rolled over the paving stones, he thought he heard a voice which was so low that he could hardly hear the words, saying, "You poor fool! You decided to do as you please, but you'll be sorry for it!"

Pinocchio was frightened, and looked around to see where these words came from, but he could see nothing. The donkeys galloped, the stage-coach rolled over the stones, and the boys inside slept. Candlewick snored like a bear; and the little man sang between his teeth,

> All sleep through the night
> But I don't sleep ...

A little way farther on Pinocchio heard again the low voice saying, "Remember this, you fool—boys who won't study, and who desert their school, their books, and their masters, always come to a bad end. I have tried it, and I know what I am talking about. The day will come when you will weep as I am weeping now; but then it will be too late!"

When he heard these whispered words, the puppet was more frightened that ever. He jumped down from the donkey's back, and took him by the bridle.

Imagine his surprise when he saw that the donkey was crying, just like a boy.

"Hullo, little man," Pinocchio called the driver. "Did you ever see such a thing? This donkey is crying."

"Let him cry! He can laugh on Tib's Eve."

"Did you teach him to talk?"

"No, he taught himself to mumble a few words when he was in a company of trained dogs for three years."

"Poor beast!"

"Come, come!" said the little man. "Don't waste time watching a donkey cry. Get on to him again, and let us go! The night is cold and the way is long."

Pinocchio obeyed without another word. The coach rolled along again, and they arrived safely about daybreak in the Land of Boobies.

It was a country unlike any other country in the world. The population was composed entirely of boys. The oldest were fourteen, and the youngest scarcely eight years old. In the streets there was such merriment, noise, and shouting that it was enough to turn anybody's head. There were troops of boys everywhere. Some were playing with nuts, some with battledores, some with balls. Some rode velocipedes, others wooden horses. A party were playing at hide and seek, a few were chasing each other. Boys dressed in straw were eating lighted tow; some were reciting, some singing, some leaping. Some were amusing themselves with walking on their hands with their feet in the air; others were trundling hoops, or strutting about dressed as generals, wearing leaf helmets and commanding a squadron of cardboard soldiers. Some were laughing, some shouting, some were calling out; others clapped their hands, or whistled, or clucked like a hen who has just laid an egg. To sum it all up, it was such a pandemonium, such a bedlam, such an uproar, that not to be deafened it would have been necessary to stuff one's ears with cotton wool. In every square, canvas theaters had been erected, and they were crowded with boys from morning till evening. On the walls of the houses there were inscriptions written in charcoal: "Long live playthings, we will have no more schools, down with arithmetic"; and similar other fine sentiments all in bad spelling.

Pinocchio, Candlewick, and the other boys who had made the journey with the little man had scarcely set foot in the town before they were in the thick of the tumult, and I need not tell you that in a few minutes they had made acquaintance with everybody. Where could happier or more contented boys be found?

In the midst of continual games and every variety of amusement, the hours, the days, and the weeks passed like lightning.

"Oh, what a delightful life!" said Pinocchio, whenever by chance he met Candlewick.

"See, then, if I was not right?" replied the other. "And to think that you did not want to come! To think that you had taken it into your head to return home to your Fairy, and to lose your time in studying! ... If you are this moment free from the bother of books and school, you must acknowledge that you owe it to me, to my advice and to my persuasions. It is only friends who know how to render such great services."

"It is true, Candlewick! If I am now a really happy boy, it is all your doing. But do you know what the master used to say when he talked to me of you? He always said to me: 'Do not associate with that rascal Candlewick, for he is a bad companion, and will only lead you into mischief!' "

"Poor master!" replied the other, shaking his head. "I know only too well that he disliked me, and amused himself by calumniating me; but I am generous and I forgive him!"

"Noble soul!" said Pinocchio, embracing his friend affectionately and kissing him between the eyes.

This delightful life had gone on for five months. The days had been entirely spent in play and amusement, without a thought of books or school, when one morning Pinocchio awoke to a most disagreeable surprise that put him into a very bad humor.

Chapter XXXII

PINOCCHIO *gets donkey's ears; and then he becomes a real little donkey and begins to bray*

What was this surprise?

I will tell you, my dear little readers. The surprise was that Pinocchio when he awoke scratched his head; and in scratching his head he discovered . . . Can you guess in the least what he discovered?

He discovered to his great astonishment that his ears had grown more than a hand.

You know that the puppet from his birth had such very small ears that they were not visible to the naked eye. You can imagine, then, what he felt when he found that during the night his ears had become so long that they seemed like two brooms.

He went at once in search of a glass that he might look at himself, but not being able to find one he filled the basin of his washing stand with water, and he saw reflected what he certainly would never have wished to see. He saw his head embellished with a magnificent pair of donkey's ears!

Only think of poor Pinocchio's sorrow, shame, and despair!

He began to cry and roar, and he beat his head against the wall; but the more he cried the longer his ears grew; they grew, and grew, and became hairy toward the points.

At the sound of his loud outcries a beautiful little Marmot that lived on the first floor came into the room. Seeing the puppet in such grief, she asked earnestly:

"What has happened to you, my dear fellow lodger?"

"I am ill, my dear little Marmot, very ill . . . and of an illness that frightens me. Do you understand counting a pulse?"

"A little."

"Then feel and see if by chance I have fever."

The little Marmot raised her right forepaw; and after having felt Pinocchio's pulse she said to him, sighing:

"My friend, I am grieved to be obliged to give you bad news!"

"What is it?"

"You have got a very bad fever!"

"What fever is it?"

"It is donkey fever."

"That is a fever that I do not understand," said the puppet, but he understood it only too well.

"Then I will explain it to you," said the Marmot. "You must know that in two or three hours you will be no longer a puppet, or a boy . . ."

"Then what shall I be?"

"In two or three hours you will become really and truly a little donkey, like those that draw carts and carry cabbages and salad to market."

"Oh, unfortunate that I am! Unfortunate that I am!" cried Pinocchio, seizing his two ears with his hands, and pulling them and tearing them furiously as if they had been someone else's ears.

"My dear boy," said the Marmot, by way of consoling him, "what can you do to prevent it? It is destiny. It is written in the decrees of wisdom that all boys who are lazy, and who take a dislike to books, to schools, and to masters, and who pass their time in amusement, games, and diversions, must end sooner or later by becoming transformed into so many little donkeys."

"But is it really so?" asked the puppet, sobbing.

"It is indeed only too true! And tears are now useless. You should have thought of it sooner!"

"But it was not my fault: believe me, little Marmot, the fault was all Candlewick's!"

"And who is this Candlewick?"

"One of my schoolfellows. I wanted to return home: I wanted to be obedient. I wished to study and earn a good character . . . but Candlewick said to me: 'Why should you bother yourself by studying? Why should you go to school? . . . Come with us instead to the Land of Boobies: there we shall none of us have to learn; there we shall amuse ourselves from morning to night, and we shall always be merry.' "

"And why did you follow the advice of that false friend—of that bad companion?"

"Why? . . . Because, my dear little Marmot, I am a puppet with no sense . . . and with no heart. Ah, if I had had the least heart I should never have left that good Fairy who loved me like a mamma, and who had done so much for me! . . . And I should be no longer a puppet . . . for I should by this time have become a little boy like so many others. But if I meet Candlewick, woe to him! He shall hear what I think of him!"

And he turned to go out. But when he reached the door he remembered his donkey's ears, and feeling ashamed to show them in public, what do you think he did? He took a big cotton cap, and putting it on his head he pulled it well down over the point of his nose.

He then set out, and went everywhere in search of Candlewick. He looked for him in the streets, in the squares, in the little theaters, in every possible place; but he could not find him. He inquired for him of everybody he met, but no one had seen him.

He then went to seek him at his house; and having reached the door, he knocked.

"Who is there?" asked Candlewick from within.

"It is I!" answered the puppet.

"Wait a moment and I will let you in."

After half an hour the door was opened, and imagine Pinocchio's feelings when upon going into the room he saw his friend Candlewick with a big cotton cap on his head which came down over his nose.

At the sight of the cap Pinocchio felt almost consoled, and thought to himself:

"Has my friend got the same illness that I have? Is he also suffering from donkey fever?"

And pretending to have observed nothing, he asked him, smiling:

"How are you, my dear Candlewick?"

"Very well; as well as a mouse in a Parmesan cheese."

"Are you saying that seriously?"

"Why should I tell you a lie?"

"Excuse me; but why, then, do you keep that cotton cap on your head which covers up your ears?"

"The doctor ordered me to wear it because I have hurt this knee. And you, dear puppet, why have you got on that cotton cap pulled down over your nose?"

"The doctor prescribed it because I have grazed my foot."

"Oh, poor Pinocchio!"

"Oh, poor Candlewick!"

After these words a long silence followed, during which the two friends did nothing but look mockingly at each other.

At last the puppet said in a soft mellifluous voice to his companion:

"Satisfy my curiosity, my dear Candlewick: have you ever suffered from disease of the ears?"

"Never! . . . And you?"

"Never! Only since this morning one of my ears aches."

"Mine is also paining me."

"You also? . . . And which of your ears hurts you?"

"Both of them. And you?"

"Both of them. Can we have gotten the same illness?"

"I fear so."

"Will you do me a kindness, Candlewick?"

"Willingly! With all my heart."

"Will you let me see your ears?"

"Why not? But first, my dear Pinocchio, I should like to see yours."

"No: you must be first."

"No, dear: first you and then I!"

"Well," said the puppet, "let us come to an agreement like good friends."

"Let us hear it."

"We will both take off our caps at the same moment. Do you agree?"

"I agree."

"Then, attention!"

And Pinocchio began to count in a loud voice:

"One! Two! Three!"

At the word Three! the two boys took off their caps and threw them into the air.

And then a scene followed that would seem incredible if it was not true. That is, when Pinocchio and Candlewick discovered that they were both struck with the same misfortune, instead of feeling full of mortification and grief, they began to prick their ungainly ears and to make a thousand antics, and they ended by going into bursts of laughter.

And they laughed, and laughed, and laughed, until they had to hold themselves together. But in the midst of their merriment, Candlewick suddenly stopped, staggered, and changing color, said to his friend:

"Help, help, Pinocchio!"

"What is the matter with you?"

"Alas, I cannot any longer stand upright."

"No more can I," exclaimed Pinocchio, tottering and beginning to cry.

And while they were talking they both doubled up and began to run around the room on their hands and feet. And as they ran, their hands became hoofs, their faces lengthened into muzzles, and their backs became covered with a light-gray hairy coat sprinkled with black.

But do you know what was the worst moment for these two wretched boys? The worst and the most humiliating moment was when their tails grew. Vanquished by shame and sorrow, they wept and lamented their fate.

Oh, if they had but been wiser! But instead of sighs and lamentations they could only bray like asses; and they brayed loudly and said in chorus: "J-a, j-a, j-a."

While this was going on someone knocked at the door, and a voice on the outside said:

"Open the door! I am the little man, I am the coachman who brought you to this country. Open at once, or it will be the worse for you!"

Chapter XXXIII

PINOCCHIO, *having become a genuine little donkey, is taken to be sold, and is bought by the director of a company of buffoons to be taught to dance, and to jump through hoops, but one evening he lames himself, and then he is bought by a man who wishes to make a drum of his skin*

Finding that the door remained shut, the little man burst it open with a violent kick, and coming into the room he said to Pinocchio and Candlewick with his usual little laugh:

"Well done, boys! You brayed well, and I recognized you by your voices. That is why I am here."

At these words the two little donkeys were quite stupefied, and stood with their heads down, their ears lowered, and their tails between their legs.

At first the little man stroked and caressed them; then taking out a currycomb he currycombed them well. And when by this process he had polished them till they shone like two mirrors, he put a halter round their necks and led them to the market place, in hope of selling them and making a good profit.

And indeed buyers were not wanting. Candlewick was bought by a peasant whose donkey had died the previous day. Pinocchio was sold to the director of a company of buffoons and tightrope dancers, who bought him that he might teach him to leap and to dance with the other animals belonging to the company.

And now, my little readers, you will have understood the fine trade that little man pursued. The wicked little monster, who had a face all milk and honey, made frequent journeys round the world with his coach. As he went along he collected, with promises and flattery, all the idle boys who had taken an aversion to books and school. As soon as his coach was full he conducted them to the Land of Boobies, that they might pass their time in games, in uproar, and in amusement. When these poor deluded boys, from continual play and no study, had become so many little donkeys, he took possession of them with great delight and satisfaction and carried them off to the fairs and markets to be sold. And in this way he had in a few years made heaps of money and had become a millionaire.

What became of Candlewick I do not know; but I do know that Pinocchio from the very first day had to endure a very hard, laborious life.

When he was put into his stall, his master filled the manger with straw; but Pinocchio, having tried a mouthful, spat it out again.

Then his master, grumbling, filled the manger with hay; but neither did the hay please him.

"Ah!" exclaimed his master in a passion. "Does not hay please you either? Leave it to me, my fine donkey; if you are so full of caprices, I will find a way to cure you!"

And by way of correcting him he struck his legs with his whip.

Pinocchio began to cry and to bray with pain, and he said, braying:

"J-a, j-a, I cannot digest straw!"

"Then eat hay!" said his master, who understood perfectly the asinine dialect.

"J-a, j-a, hay gives me a pain in my stomach."

"Do you mean to pretend that a little donkey like you must be kept on breasts of chickens, and capons in jelly?"

asked his master, getting more and more angry, and whipping him again.

At this second whipping Pinocchio prudently held his tongue and said nothing more.

The stable was then shut and Pinocchio was left alone. He had not eaten for many hours, and he began to yawn from hunger. And when he yawned he opened a mouth that seemed as wide as an oven.

At last, finding nothing else in the manger, he resigned himself, and chewed a little hay; and after he had chewed it well, he shut his eyes and swallowed it.

"This hay is not bad," he said to himself, "but how much better it would have been if I had gone on with my studies! Instead of hay I might now be eating a hunch of new bread and a fine slice of sausage. But I must have patience! . . ."

The next morning when he woke he looked in the manger for a little more hay; but he found none, for he had eaten it all during the night.

Then he took a mouthful of chopped straw; but while he was chewing it he had to acknowledge that the taste of chopped straw did not in the least resemble a savory dish of macaroni or rice.

"But I must have patience!" he repeated as he went on chewing. "May my example serve at least as a warning to all disobedient boys who do not want to study. Patience! . . . Patience! . . ."

"Patience, indeed!" shouted his master, coming at that moment into the stable. "Do you think, my little donkey, that I bought you only to give you food and drink? I bought you to make you work, and that you might earn money for me. Up, then, at once! You must come with me into the circus, and there I will teach you to jump through hoops, to go through frames of paper head foremost, to dance waltzes and polkas, and to stand upright on your hind legs."

Poor Pinocchio, either by love or by force, had to learn all these fine things. But it took him three months before

he had learnt them, and he got many a whipping that
nearly took off his skin.

At last a day came when his master was able to an-
nounce that he would give a really extraordinary representation. The many-colored placards stuck on the street
corners were thus worded:

GREAT FULL-DRESS REPRESENTATION
————

TONIGHT
WILL TAKE PLACE THE USUAL FEATS
AND SURPRISING PERFORMANCES
EXECUTED BY ALL THE ARTISTES
AND BY ALL THE HORSES OF THE COMPANY
AND MOREOVER
THE FAMOUS
LITTLE DONKEY PINOCCHIO
CALLED
THE STAR OF THE DANCE
WILL MAKE HIS FIRST APPEARANCE
————

THE THEATER WILL BE BRILLIANTLY ILLUMINATED

On that evening, as you may imagine, an hour before
the play was to begin the theater was crammed.

There was not a place to be had either in the pit or in
the stalls, or in the boxes even, by paying its weight in
gold.

The benches round the circus were crowded with children and with boys of all ages, who were in a fever of im-
patience to see the famous little donkey Pinocchio dance.

When the first part of the performance was over, the director of the company, dressed in a black coat, white
shorts, and big leather boots that came above his knees,
presented himself to the public, and after making a profound bow he began with much solemnity the following ridiculous speech:

"Respectable public, ladies and gentlemen! The humble

undersigned being a passer-by in this illustrious city, I have wished to procure for myself the honor, not to say the pleasure, of presenting to this intelligent and distinguished audience a celebrated little donkey, who has already had the honor of dancing in the presence of his Majesty the Emperor of all the principal courts of Europe.

"And thanking you, I beg of you to help us with your inspiring presence and to be indulgent to us."

This speech was received with much laughter and applause; but the applause redoubled and became tumultuous when the little donkey Pinocchio made his appearance in the middle of the circus. He was decked out for the occasion. He had a new bridle of polished leather with brass buckles and studs, and two white camellias in his ears. His mane was divided and curled, and each curl was tied with bows of colored ribbon. He had a girth of gold and silver round his body, and his tail was plaited with amaranth and blue velvet ribbons. He was, in fact, a little donkey to fall in love with!

The director, in presenting him to the public, added these few words:

"My respectable auditors! I am not here to tell you falsehoods of the great difficulties that I have overcome in understanding and subjugating this mammifer, while he was grazing at liberty among the mountains in the plains of the torrid zone. I beg you will observe the wild rolling of his eyes. Every means having been tried in vain to tame him, and to accustom him to the life of domestic quadrupeds, I was often forced to have recourse to the convincing argument of the whip. But all my goodness to him, instead of gaining his affections, has, on the contrary, increased his viciousness. However, following the system of Gall, I discovered in his cranium a bony cartilage, that the Faculty of Medicine in Paris has itself recognized as the regenerating bulb of the hair, and of dance. For this reason I have not only taught him to dance, but also to jump through hoops and through frames covered with paper. Admire him, and then pass your opinion on him! But be-

fore taking my leave of you, permit me, ladies and gentlemen, to invite you to the daily performance that will take
place tomorrow evening; but in the apotheosis that the
weather should threaten rain, the performance will be post-
poned till tomorrow morning at eleven antemeridian of
postmeridian."

Here the director made another profound bow; and then
turning to Pinocchio, he said:

"Courage, Pinocchio! Before you begin your feats make
your bow to this distinguished audience—ladies, gentlemen, and children."

Pinocchio obeyed, and bent both his knees till they
touched the ground, and remained kneeling until the director, cracking his whip, shouted to him:

"At a foot's pace!"

Then the little donkey raised himself on his four legs
and began to walk round the theater, keeping at a foot's
pace.

After a little the director cried:

"Trot!" and Pinocchio, obeying the order, changed to a
trot.

"Gallop!" and Pinocchio went full gallop. But while he
was going full speed like a race horse, the director, raising
his arm in the air, fired off a pistol.

At the shot the little donkey, pretending to be wounded,
fell his whole length in the circus, as if he were really
dying.

As he got up from the ground amid an outburst of applause, shouts, and clapping of hands, he naturally raised
his head and looked up ... and he saw in one of the boxes
a beautiful lady who wore round her neck a thick gold
chain from which hung a medallion. On the medallion was
painted the portrait of a puppet.

"That is my portrait! ... That lady is the Fairy!" said
Pinocchio to himself, recognizing her immediately; and
overcome with delight he tried to cry:

"Oh, my little Fairy! Oh, my little Fairy!"

But instead of these words a bray came from his throat,

so sonorous and so prolonged that all the spectators laughed, and more especially all the children who were in the theater.

Then the director, to teach him a lesson, and to make him understand that it is not good manners to bray before the public, gave him a blow on his nose with the handle of his whip.

The poor little donkey put his tongue out an inch, and licked his nose for at least five minutes, thinking perhaps that it would ease the pain he felt.

But what was his despair when, looking up a second time, he saw that the box was empty and that the Fairy had disappeared!

He thought he was going to die; his eyes filled with tears and he began to weep. Nobody, however, noticed it, and least of all the director who, cracking his whip, shouted:

"Courage, Pinocchio! Now let the audience see how gracefully you can jump through the hoops."

Pinocchio tried two or three times, but each time that he came in front of the hoop, instead of going through it, he found it easier to go under it. At last he made a leap and went through it; but his right leg unfortunately caught in the hoop, and that cause him to fall to the ground doubled up in a heap on the other side.

When he got up he was lame, and it was only with great difficulty that he managed to return to the stable.

"Bring out Pinocchio! We want the little donkey! Bring out the little donkey!" shouted all the boys in the theater, touched and sorry for the sad accident.

But the little donkey was seen no more that evening.

The following morning the veterinary, that is, the doctor of animals, paid him a visit, and declared that he would remain lame for life.

The director then said to the stableboy:

"What do you suppose I can do with a lame donkey? He would eat food without earning it. Take him to the market and sell him."

When they reached the market a purchaser was found at once. He asked the stableboy:

"How much do you want for that lame donkey?"

"Twenty francs."

"I will give you twenty pence. Don't suppose that I am buying him to make use of; I am buying him solely for his skin. I see that his skin is very hard, and I intend to make a drum with it for the band of my village."

I leave it to my readers to imagine poor Pinocchio's feelings when he heard that he was destined to become a drum!

As soon as the purchaser had paid his twenty pence he conducted the little donkey to the seashore. He then put a stone round his neck, and tying a rope, the end of which he held in his hand, round his leg, he gave him a sudden push and threw him into the water.

Pinocchio, weighed down by the stone, went at once to the bottom; and his owner, keeping tight hold of the cord, sat down quietly on a piece of rock to wait until the little donkey was drowned, intending then to skin him.

Chapter XXXIV

PINOCCHIO, *having been thrown into the sea, is eaten by the fish and becomes a puppet as he was before. While he is swimming away to save his life he is swallowed by the terrible* DOGFISH

After Pinocchio had been fifty minutes under the water, his purchaser said aloud to himself:

"My poor little lame donkey must by this time be quite drowned. I will therefore pull him out of the water, and I will make a fine drum of his skin."

And he began to haul in the rope that he had tied to the donkey's leg; and he hauled, and hauled, and hauled, until at last . . . what do you think appeared above the water? Instead of a little dead donkey he saw a live puppet, who was wriggling like an eel.

Seeing this wooden puppet, the poor man thought he was dreaming, and, struck dumb with astonishment, he remained with his mouth open and his eyes starting out of his head.

Having somewhat recovered from his first stupefaction, he asked in a quavering voice:

"And the little donkey that I threw into the sea? What has become of him?"

"I am the little donkey!" said Pinocchio, laughing.

"You?"

"I."

"Ah, you young scamp! Do you dare to make game of me?"

"To make game of you? Quite the contrary, my dear master; I am speaking seriously."

"But how can you, who, but a short time ago, were a little donkey, have become a wooden puppet, only from having been left in the water?"

"It must have been the effect of sea water. The sea makes extraordinary changes."

"Beware, puppet, beware! ... Don't imagine that you can amuse yourself at my expense. Woe to you, if I lose patience!"

"Well, master, do you wish to know the true story? If you will set my leg free I will tell it you."

The good man, who was curious to hear the true story, immediately untied the knot that kept him bound; and Pinocchio, finding himself free as a bird in the air, commenced as follows:

"You must know that I was once a puppet as I am now, and I was on the point of becoming a boy like the many that there are in the world. But instead, induced by my dislike to study and the advice of bad companions, I ran away from home ... and one fine day when I awoke I found myself changed into a donkey with long ears ... and a long tail! What a disgrace it was to me!—a disgrace, dear master, that the blessed St. Anthony would not inflict even upon you! Taken to the market to be sold, I was bought by the director of an equestrian company, who took it into his head to make a famous dancer of me, and a famous leaper through hoops. But one night during a performance I had a bad fall in the circus and lamed both my legs. Then the director, not knowing what to do with a lame donkey, sent me to be sold, and you were the purchaser!"

"Only too true! And I paid twenty pence for you. And now who will give me back my poor pennies?"

"And why did you buy me? You bought me to make a drum of my skin! ... A drum!"

"Only too true! And now where shall I find another skin?"

"Don't despair, master. There are such a number of little donkeys in the world!"

"Tell me, you impertinent rascal, does your story end here?"

"No," answered the puppet. "I have another two words to say and then I shall have finished. After you had bought me you brought me to this place to kill me; but then, yielding to a feeling of compassion, you preferred to tie a stone round my neck and to throw me into the sea. This humane feeling does you great honor, and I shall always be grateful to you for it. But nevertheless, dear master, this time you made your calculations without considering the Fairy!"

"And who is this Fairy?"

"She is my mamma, and she resembles all other good mammas who care for their children, and who never lose sight of them, but help them lovingly, even when, on account of their foolishness and evil conduct, they deserve to be abandoned and left to themselves. Well, then, the good Fairy, as soon as she saw that I was in danger of drowning, sent immediately an immense shoal of fish, who, believing me really to be a little dead donkey, began to eat me. And what mouthfuls they took: I should never have thought that fish were greedier than boys! ... Some ate my ears, some my muzzle, others my neck and mane, some the skin of my legs, some my coat ... and among them there was a little fish so polite that he even condescended to eat my tail."

"From this time forth," said his purchaser, horrified, "I swear that I will never touch fish. It would be too dreadful to open a mullet, or a fried whiting, and to find inside a donkey's tail!"

"I agree with you," said the puppet, laughing. "However, I must tell you that when the fish had finished eating the donkey's hide that covered me from head to foot, they naturally reached the bone . . . or rather the wood, for as you see I am made of the hardest wood. But after giving a few bites they soon discovered that I was not a morsel for their teeth, and, disgusted with such indigestible food, they went off, some in one direction and some in another, without so much as saying thank you to me. And now, at last, I have told you how it was that when you pulled up the rope you found a live puppet instead of a dead donkey."

"I laugh at your story," cried the man in a rage. "I know only that I spent twenty pence to buy you, and I will have my money back. Shall I tell you what I will do? I will take you back to the market and I will sell you by weight as seasoned wood for lighting fires."

"Sell me if you like; I am content," said Pinocchio.

But as he said it he made a spring and plunged into the water. Swimming gaily away from the shore, he called to his poor owner:

"Good-by, master. If you should be in want of a skin to make a drum, remember me."

And he laughed and went on swimming; and after a while he turned again and shouted louder:

"Good-by, master. If you should be in want of a little well-seasoned wood for lighting the fire, remember me."

In the twinkling of an eye he had swum so far off that he was scarcely visible. All that could be seen of him was a little black speck on the surface of the sea that from time to time lifted its legs out of the water and leapt and capered like a dolphin enjoying himself.

While Pinocchio was swimming, he knew not whither, he saw in the midst of the sea a rock that seemed to be made of white marble, and on the summit there stood a beautiful little goat who bleated lovingly and made signs to him to approach.

But the most singular thing was this: The little goat's hair, instead of being white or black, or a mixture of two colors as is usual with other goats, was blue, and of a very vivid blue, greatly resembling the hair of the beautiful Child.

I leave you to imagine how rapidly poor Pinocchio's heart began to beat. He swam with redoubled strength and energy towards the white rock; and he was already half-way when he saw, rising up out of the water and coming to meet him, the horrible head of a sea monster. His wide-open cavernous mouth and his three rows of enormous teeth would have been terrifying to look at even in a picture.

And do you know what this sea monster was?

This sea monster was neither more nor less than that gigantic Dogfish who has been mentioned many times in this story, and who, for his slaughter and for his insatiable voracity, had been named the "Attila of Fish and Fishermen."

Only think of poor Pinocchio's terror at the sight of the monster. He tried to avoid it, to change his direction; he tried to escape; but that immense wide-open mouth came toward him with the velocity of an arrow.

"Be quick, Pinocchio, for pity's sake," cried the beautiful little goat, bleating.

And Pinocchio swam desperately with his arms, his chest, his legs, and his feet.

"Quick, Pinocchio, the monster is close upon you!"

And Pinocchio swam quicker than ever, and flew on with the rapidity of a ball from a gun. He had nearly reached the rock, and the little goat, leaning over toward the sea, had stretched out her forelegs to help him out of the water . . .

But it was too late! The monster had overtaken him, and drawing in his breath, he sucked in the poor puppet as he would have sucked a hen's egg; and he swallowed him with such violence and avidity that Pinocchio, in falling into the Dogfish's stomach, received such a blow that he remained unconscious for a quarter of an hour afterward.

When he came to himself again after the shock he could not in the least imagine in what world he was. All around him it was quite dark, and the darkness was so black and so profound that it seemed to him that he had fallen head downward into an inkstand full of ink. He listened, but he could hear no noise; only from time to time great gusts of wind blew in his face. At first he could not understand where the wind came from, but at last he discovered that it came out of the monster's lungs. For you must know that the Dogfish suffered very much from asthma, and when he breathed it was exactly as if a north wind was blowing.

Pinocchio at first tried to keep up his courage; but when he had one proof after another that he was really shut up in the body of the sea monster he began to cry and scream and to sob out:

"Help! Help! Oh, how unfortunate I am! Will nobody come to save me?"

"Who do you think could save you, unhappy wretch?" said a voice in the dark that sounded like a guitar out of tune.

"Who is speaking?" asked Pinocchio, frozen with terror.

"It is I! I am a poor Tunny who was swallowed by the Dogfish at the same time that you were. And what fish are you?"

"I have nothing in common with fish. I am a puppet."

"Then if you are not a fish, why did you let yourself be swallowed by the monster?"

"I didn't let myself be swallowed: it was the monster that swallowed me! And now, what are we to do here in the dark?"

"Resign ourselves and wait until the Dogfish has digested us both."

"But I do not want to be digested!" howled Pinocchio, beginning to cry again.

"Neither do I want to be digested," added the Tunny; "but I am enough of a philosopher to console myself by thinking that when one is born a Tunny it is more dignified to die in the water than in oil."

"That is all nonsense!" cried Pinocchio.

"It is my opinion," replied the Tunny, "and opinions, so say the political Tunnies, ought to be respected."

"To sum it all up . . . I want to get away from here . . . I want to escape."

"Escape if you are able!"

"Is this Dogfish who has swallowed us very big?" asked the puppet.

"Big! Why, only imagine, his body is two miles long without counting his tail."

While they were holding this conversation in the dark, Pinocchio thought that he saw a light a long way off.

"What is that little light I see in the distance?" he asked.

"It is most likely some companion in misfortune who is waiting like us to be digested."

"I will go and find him. Do you not think that it may by chance be some old fish who perhaps could show us how to escape?"

"I hope it may be so with all my heart, dear puppet."

"Good-by, Tunny."

"Good-by, puppet, and good fortune attend you."

"Where shall we meet again?"

"Who can say? . . . It is better not even to think of it!"

Chapter XXXV

PINOCCHIO *finds in the body of the* DOGFISH ...
*whom does he find? Read this chapter and you
will know*

Pinocchio, having taken leave of his friend the Tunny,
began to grope his way in the dark through the body
of the Dogfish, taking a step at a time in the direction of
the light that he saw shining dimly at a great distance.

The farther he advanced the brighter became the light;
and he walked and walked until at last he reached it; and
when he reached it ... what did he find? I will give you
a thousand guesses. He found a little table spread out, and
on it a lighted candle stuck into a green glass bottle, and
seated at the table was a little old man. He was eating
some live fish, and they were so very much alive that
while he was eating them they sometimes even jumped out
of his mouth.

At this sight Pinocchio was filled with such great and
unexpected joy that he became almost delirious. He
wanted to laugh, he wanted to cry, he wanted to say a
thousand things, and instead he could only stammer out a
few confused and broken words. At last he succeeded in

uttering a cry of joy, and opening his arms he threw them
around the little old man's neck, and began to shout:

"Oh, my dear papa! I have found you at last! I will
never leave you more, never more, never more!"

"Then my eyes tell me true?" said the little old man,
rubbing his eyes. "Then you are really my dear
Pinocchio?"

"Yes, yes, I am Pinocchio, really Pinocchio! And you
have quite forgiven me, have you not? Oh, my dear papa,
how good you are ... and to think that I, on the contrary ... Oh, but if you only knew what misfortunes have
been poured on my head, and all that has befallen me!
Only imagine, the day that you, poor dear papa, sold your
coat to buy me a spelling book that I might go to school,
I escaped to see the puppet show, and the showman
wanted to put me on the fire that I might roast his mutton,
and it was he who afterwards gave me five gold pieces to
take them to you, but I met the Fox and the Cat, who took
me to the inn of the Red Crawfish, where they ate like
wolves, and I left by myself in the middle of the night, and
I encountered assassins who ran after me, and I ran away,
and they followed, and I ran, and they always followed
me, and I ran, until they hung me to a branch of a Big
Oak, and the beautiful Child with blue hair sent a little
carriage to fetch me, and the doctors when they had seen
me said immediately: 'If he is not dead, it is proof that he
is still alive'—and then by chance I told a lie, and my nose
began to grow until I could no longer get through the door
of the room, for which reason I went with the Fox and the
Cat to bury the four gold pieces, for one I had spent at the
inn, and the Parrot began to laugh, and instead of two
thousand gold pieces I found none left, for which reason
the judge when he heard that I had been robbed had me
immediately put in prison to content the robbers, and then
when I was coming away I saw a beautiful bunch of
grapes in a field, and I was caught in a trap, and the peasant, who was quite right, put a dog collar round my neck
that I might guard the poultry yard, and acknowledging

my innocence let me go, and the Serpent with the smoking tail began to laugh and broke a blood vessel in his chest, and so I returned to the house of the beautiful Child who was dead, and the Pigeon, seeing that I was crying, said to me, 'I have seen your father who was building a little boat to go in search of you,' and I said to him, 'Oh, if I also had wings!' and he said to me, 'Do you want to go to your father?' and I said, 'Without doubt! But who will take me to him?' and he said to me, 'I will take you,' and I said to him, 'How?' and he said to me, 'Get on my back,' and so we flew all night, and then in the morning all the fishermen who were looking out to sea said to me, 'There is a poor man in a boat who is on the point of being drowned,' and I recognized you at once, even at that distance, for my heart told me, and I made signs to you to return to land . . ."

"I also recognized you," said Geppetto, "and I would willingly have returned to the shore: but what was I to do? The sea was tremendous, and a great wave upset my boat. Then a horrible Dogfish who was near, as soon as he saw me in the water, came toward me, and putting out his tongue took hold of me, and swallowed me as if I had been a little Bologna tart."

"And how long have you been shut up here?" asked Pinocchio.

"Since that day—it must be nearly two years ago: two years, my dear Pinocchio, that have seemed like two centuries!"

"And how have you managed to live? And where did you get the candle? And the matches to light it? Who gave them to you?"

"Stop, and I will tell you everything. You must know, then, that in the same storm in which my boat was upset a merchant vessel foundered. The sailors were all saved, but the vessel went to the bottom, and the Dogfish, who had that day an excellent appetite, after he had swallowed me, swallowed also the vessel . . ."

"How?"

"He swallowed it in one mouthful, and the only thing that he spat out was the mainmast, that had stuck between his teeth like a fishbone. Fortunately for me the vessel was laden with preserved meat in tins, biscuits, bottles of wine, dried raisins, cheese, coffee, sugar, candles, and boxes of wax matches. With this providential supply I have been able to live for two years. But I have arrived at the end of my resources; there is nothing left in the larder, and this candle that you see burning is the last that remains . . ."

"And after that?"

"After that, dear boy, we shall both remain in the dark."

"Then, dear little papa," said Pinocchio, "there is no time to lose. We must think of escaping."

"Of escaping? . . . And how?"

"We must escape through the mouth of the Dogfish, throw ourselves into the sea and swim away."

"You talk well: but, dear Pinocchio, I don't know how to swim."

"What does that matter? I am a good swimmer, and you can get on my shoulders and I will carry you safely to shore."

"All illusions, my boy!" replied Geppetto, shaking his head, with a melancholy smile. "Do you suppose it possible that a puppet like you, scarcely a meter high, could have the strength to swim with me on his shoulders!"

"Try it and you will see!"

Without another word Pinocchio took the candle in his hand, and going in front to light the way, he said to his father:

"Follow me, and don't be afraid."

And they walked for some time and traversed the body and the stomach of the Dogfish. But when they arrived at the point where the monster's big throat began, they thought it better to stop to give a good look around and to choose the best moment for escaping.

Now I must tell you that the Dogfish, being very old, and suffering from asthma and palpitation of the heart, was obliged to sleep with his mouth open. Pinocchio, therefore, having approached the entrance to his throat and, looking up, could see beyond the enormous gaping mouth a large piece of starry sky and beautiful moonlight.

"This is the moment to escape," he whispered, turning to his father. "The Dogfish is sleeping like a dormouse, the sea is calm, and it is as light as day. Follow me, dear papa, and in a short time we shall be in safety."

They immediately climbed up the throat of the sea monster, and having reached his immense mouth they began to walk on tiptoe down his tongue.

Before taking the final leap the puppet said to his father:

"Get on my shoulders and put your arms tight around my neck. I will take care of the rest."

As soon as Geppetto was firmly settled on his son's shoulders, Pinocchio, feeling sure of himself, threw himself into the water and began to swim. The sea was as smooth as oil, the moon shone brilliantly, and the Dogfish was sleeping so profoundly that even a cannonade would have failed to wake him.

Chapter XXXVI

PINOCCHIO *at last ceases to be a puppet and becomes a boy*

While Pinocchio was swimming quickly toward the shore he discovered that his father, who was on his shoulders with his legs in the water, was trembling as violently as if the poor man had got an attack of ague fever.

Was he trembling from cold or from fear? Perhaps a little from both the one and the other. But Pinocchio, thinking that it was from fear, said to comfort him:

"Courage, Papa! In a few minutes we shall be safely on shore."

"But where is this blessed shore?" asked the little old man, becoming still more frightened, and screwing up his eyes as tailors do when they wish to thread a needle. "I have been looking in every direction and I see nothing but the sky and the sea."

"But I see the shore as well," said the puppet. "You must know that I am like a cat: I see better by night than by day."

Poor Pinocchio was making a pretense of being in good spirits, but in reality . . . in reality he was beginning to feel discouraged; his strength was failing, he was gasping and panting for breath ... he could do no more, and the shore was still far off.

He swam until he had no breath left; then he turned his head to Geppetto and said in broken words:

"Papa ... help me ... I am dying!"

The father and son were on the point of drowning when they heard a voice like a guitar out of tune saying:

"Who is it that is dying?"

"It is I, and my poor father!"

"I know that voice! You are Pinocchio!"

"Precisely; and you?"

"I am the Tunny, your prison companion in the body of the Dogfish."

"And how did you manage to escape?"

"I followed your example. You showed me the road, and I escaped after you."

"Tunny, you have arrived at the right moment! I implore you to help us, or we are lost."

"Willingly and with all my heart. You must, both of you, take hold of my tail and allow me to guide you. I will take you on shore in four minutes."

Geppetto and Pinocchio, as I need not tell you, accepted the offer at once; but instead of holding on by his tail they thought it would be more comfortable to get on the Tunny's back.

Having reached the shore, Pinocchio sprang first on land that he might help his father to do the same. He then turned to the Tunny, and said to him in a voice full of emotion:

"My friend, you have saved my papa's life. I can find no words with which to thank you properly. Permit me at least to give you a kiss as a sign of my eternal gratitude!"

The Tunny put his head out of the water, and Pinocchio, kneeling on the ground, kissed him tenderly on the mouth. At this spontaneous proof of warm affection, the poor Tunny, who was not accustomed to it, felt extremely touched, and ashamed to let himself be seen crying like a child, he plunged under the water and disappeared.

By this time the day had dawned. Pinocchio, then offering his arm to Geppetto, who had scarcely breath to stand, said to him:

"Lean on my arm, dear papa, and let us go. We will walk very slowly like the ants, and when we are tired we can rest by the wayside."

"And where shall we go?" asked Geppetto.

"In search of some house or cottage, where they will give us for charity a mouthful of bread, and a little straw to serve as a bed."

They had not gone a hundred yards when they saw by the roadside two villainous-looking individuals begging.

They were the Cat and the Fox, but they were scarcely recognizable. Fancy! The Cat had so long feigned blindness that she had become blind in reality; and the Fox, old, mangy, and with one side paralyzed, had not even his tail left. That sneaking thief, having fallen into the most squalid misery, one fine day had found himself obliged to sell his beautiful tail to a traveling peddler, who bought it to drive away flies.

"Oh, Pinocchio!" cried the Fox. "Give a little in charity to two poor infirm people."

"Infirm people," repeated the Cat.

"Begone, impostors!" answered the puppet. "You took me in once, but you will never catch me again."

"Believe me, Pinocchio, we are now poor and unfortunate indeed!"

"If you are poor, you deserve it. Recollect the proverb: 'Stolen money never fructifies.' Begone, imposters!"

And thus saying Pinocchio and Geppetto went their way in peace. When they had gone another hundred yards they saw, at the end of a path in the middle of the fields, a nice little straw hut with a roof of tiles and bricks.

"That hut must be inhabited by someone," said Pinocchio. "Let us go and knock at the door."

They went and knocked.

"Who is there?" said a little voice from within.

"We are a poor father and son without bread and without a roof," answered the puppet.

"Turn the key and the door will open," said the same little voice.

Pinocchio turned the key and the door opened. They went in and looked here, there, and everywhere, but could see no one.

"Oh, where is the master of the house?" said Pinocchio, much surprised.

"Here I am up here!"

The father and son looked immediately up to the ceiling, and there on a beam they saw the Talking Cricket.

"Oh, my dear little Cricket!" said Pinocchio, bowing politely to him.

"Ah! Now you call me your 'dear little Cricket.' But do you remember the time when you threw the handle of a hammer at me, to drive me from your house?"

"You are right, Cricket! Drive me away also ... throw the handle of a hammer at me; but have pity on my poor papa ..."

"I will have pity on both father and son, but I wished to remind you of the ill treatment I received from you, to teach you that in this world, when it is possible, we should show courtesy to everybody, if we wish it to be extended to us in our hour of need."

"You are right, Cricket, you are right, and I will bear in mind the lesson you have given me. But tell me how you managed to buy this beautiful hut."

"This hut was given to me yesterday by a goat whose wool was of a beautiful blue color."

"And where has the goat gone?" asked Pinocchio, with lively curiosity.

"I do not know."

"And when will it come back?"

"It will never come back. It went away yesterday in great grief and, bleating, it seemed to say: 'Poor Pinocchio ... I shall never see him more ... by this time the Dogfish must have devoured him!' "

"Did it really say that? ... Then it was she! ... It was she! ... It was my dear little Fairy!" exclaimed Pinocchio, crying and sobbing.

When he had cried for some time he dried his eyes, and prepared a comfortable bed of straw for Geppetto to lie down upon. Then he asked the Cricket:

"Tell me, little Cricket, where can I find a tumbler of milk for my poor papa?"

"Three fields off from here there lives a gardener called Giangio who keeps cows. Go to him and you will get the milk you are in want of."

Pinocchio ran all the way to Giangio's house; and the gardener asked him:

"How much milk do you want?"

"I want a tumblerful."

"A tumbler of milk costs a halfpenny. Begin by giving me the halfpenny."

"I have not even a farthing," replied Pinocchio, grieved and mortified.

"That is bad, Puppet," answered the gardener. "If you have not even a farthing, I have not even a drop of milk."

"I must have patience!" said Pinocchio, and he turned to go.

"Wait a little," said Giangio. "We can come to an arrangement together. Will you undertake to turn the pumping machine?"

"What is the pumping machine?"

"It is a wooden pole which serves to draw up the water from the cistern to water the vegetables."

"You can try me ..."

"Well, then, if you will draw a hundred buckets of water, I will give you in compensation a tumbler of milk."

"It is a bargain."

Giangio then led Pinocchio to the kitchen garden and taught him how to turn the pumping machine. Pinocchio immediately began to work; but before he had drawn up the hundred buckets of water the perspiration was pouring from his head to his feet. Never before had he undergone such fatigue.

"Up till now," said the gardener, "the labor turning the pumping machine was performed by my little donkey, but the poor animal is dying."

"Will you take me to see him?" said Pinocchio.

"Willingly."

When Pinocchio went into the stable he saw a beautiful little donkey stretched on the straw, worn out from hunger and overwork. After looking at him earnestly he said to himself, much troubled:

"I am sure I know this little donkey! His face is not new to me."

And bending over him he asked him in asinine language:

"Who are you?"

At this question the little donkey opened his dying eyes, and answered in broken words in the same language:

"I am ... Can ... dle ... wick ..."

And, having again closed his eyes, he expired.

"Oh, poor Candlewick!" said Pinocchio in a low voice; and taking a handful of straw he dried a tear that was rolling down his face.

"Do you grieve for a donkey that cost you nothing?" said the gardener. "What must it be to me who bought him for ready money?"

"I must tell you ... he was my friend!"

"Your friend?"

"One of my schoolfellows!"

"How?" shouted Giangio, laughing loudly. "How? Had you donkeys for schoolfellows? ... I can imagine what wonderful studies you must have made!"

The puppet, who felt much mortified at these words, did not answer; but taking his tumbler of milk, still quite warm, he returned to the hut.

And from that day for more than five months he continued to get up at daybreak every morning to go and turn the pumping machine, to earn the tumbler of milk that was of such benefit to his father in his bad state of health. Nor was he satisfied with this; for, during the time that he had over, he learned to make hampers and baskets of rushes, and with the money he obtained by selling them he was able with great economy to provide for all the daily expenses. Among other things he constructed an elegant little wheel chair, in which he would take his father out on fine days to breathe a mouthful of fresh air.

By his industry, ingenuity, and his anxiety to work and to overcome difficulties, he not only succeeded in maintaining his father, who continued infirm, in comfort, but he also contrived to put aside forty pence to buy himself a new coat.

One morning he said to his father:

"I am going to the neighboring market to buy myself a jacket, a cap, and a pair of shoes. When I return," he added, laughing, "I shall be so well dressed that you will take me for a fine gentleman."

And leaving the house he began to run merrily and happily along. All at once he heard himself called by name, and turning around he saw a big Snail crawling out from the hedge.

"Do you not know me?" asked the Snail.

"It seems to me . . . and yet I am not sure . . ."

"Do you not remember the Snail who was lady's maid to the Fairy with blue hair? Do you not remember the time when I came downstairs to let you in, and you were caught by your foot which you had stuck through the house door?"

"I remember it all!" shouted Pinocchio. "Tell me quickly, my beautiful little Snail, where have you left my good Fairy? What is she doing? Has she forgiven me? Does she still remember me? Does she still wish me well? Is she far from here? Can I go and see her?"

To all these rapid, breathless questions the Snail replied in her usual phlegmatic manner:

"My dear Pinocchio, the poor Fairy is lying in bed at the hospital!"

"At the hospital?"

"It is only too true. Overtaken by a thousand misfortunes, she has fallen seriously ill, and she has not even enough to buy herself a mouthful of bread."

"Is it really so? Oh, what sorrow you have given me! Oh, poor Fairy, poor Fairy, poor Fairy! . . . If I had a million I would run and carry it to her . . . but I have only forty pence . . . Here they are: I was going to buy a new coat. Take them, Snail, and carry them at once to my good Fairy."

"And your new coat?"

"What matters my new coat? I would sell even these rags that I have got on to be able to help her. Go, Snail, and be quick; and in two days return to this place, for I hope I shall then be able to give you some more money. Up to this time I have worked to maintain my papa; from today I will work five hours more that I may also maintain my good mamma. Good-by, Snail, I shall expect you in two days."

The Snail, contrary to her usual habits, began to run like a lizard in a hot August sun.

That evening Pinocchio, instead of going to bed at ten o'clock, sat up till midnight had struck; and instead of making eight baskets of rushes he made sixteen.

Then he went to bed and fell asleep. And while he slept he thought that he saw the Fairy smiling and beautiful, who, after having kissed him, said to him:

"Well done, Pinocchio! To reward you for your good heart I will forgive you for all that is past. Boys who minister tenderly to their parents, and assist them in their misery and infirmities, are deserving of great praise and affection, even if they cannot be cited as examples of obedience and good behavior. Try and do better in the future and you will be happy."

At this moment his dream ended, and Pinocchio opened his eyes and awoke.

But imagine his astonishment when upon awakening he discovered that he was no longer a wooden puppet, but that he had become instead a boy, like all other boys. He gave a glance round and saw that the straw walls of the hut had disappeared, and that he was in a pretty little room furnished and arranged with a simplicity that was almost elegance. Jumping out of bed he found a new suit of clothes ready for him, a new cap, and pair of new leather boots that fitted him beautifully.

He was hardly dressed when he naturally put his hands in his pockets, and pulled out a little ivory purse on which these words were written: "The Fairy with blue hair returns the forty pence to her dear Pinocchio, and thanks him for his good heart." He opened the purse, and instead of forty copper pennies he saw forty shining gold pieces fresh from the mint.

He then went and looked at himself in the glass, and he thought he was someone else. For he no longer saw the usual reflection of a wooden puppet; he was greeted instead by the image of a bright, intelligent boy with chestnut hair, blue eyes, and looking as happy and joyful as if it were the Easter holidays.

In the midst of all these wonders succeeding each other Pinocchio felt quite bewildered, and he could not tell if he was really awake or if he was dreaming with his eyes open.

"Where can my papa be!" he exclaimed suddenly, and going into the next room he found old Geppetto quite well, lively, and in good humor, just as he had been formerly. He had already resumed his trade of wood carving, and he was designing a rich and beautiful frame of leaves, flowers, and the heads of animals.

"Satisfy my curiosity, dear papa," said Pinocchio, throwing his arms around his neck and covering him with kisses. "How can this sudden change be accounted for?"

"This sudden change in our home is all your doing," answered Geppetto.

"How my doing?"

"Because when boys who have behaved badly turn over a new leaf and become good, they have the power of bringing contentment and happiness to their families."

"And where has the old wooden Pinocchio hidden himself?"

"There he is," answered Geppetto, and he pointed to a big puppet, leaning against a chair, with its head on one side, its arms dangling, and its legs so crossed and bent that it was really a miracle that it remained standing.

Pinocchio turned and looked at it; and after he had looked at it for a short time, he said to himself with great complacency:

"How ridiculous I was when I was a puppet! And how glad I am that I have become a well-behaved little boy!"

Afterword

From the overt "Woe to boys who revolt against their parents and run away from home," to the more subtle importance of family, *Pinocchio* touches on themes as true today as they were in Collodi's time.

One of the first lessons that Pinocchio learns is "waste not, want not" when he is starving, but won't even consider eating the peels or core of a pear. His hunger, of course, turns out to be less managable than he imagined, and he was glad to have those peels and that core after all.

This characteristic begins our introduction to Pinocchio's selfish nature. He is continually tempted by the idea of getting something for nothing. In one instance, he loses all his money and almost loses his life by going with some thieves on the promise of turning a gold coin into a tree full of gold coins.

Eventually, the ultimate temptation arrives and he goes with a bunch of other boys to "Playland," where idleness is a way of life for all youth. No work, no school, only play. And as Pinocchio finds out, when a boy isn't doing something worthwhile, then he is making an ass of himself, and so author Carlo Collodi takes this very literally and turns all the boys, eventually, into asses.

The one thing Pinocchio cannot get away with is lying, for the effects of telling even a small fib are immediate and as plain as the nose on his face.

The greatest lesson of all lies with Geppetto, whom Pinocchio finds ill and forlorn and on the verge of giving up hope of ever finding his son. Pinocchio, knowing that his behavior is the cause of his father's worry, nurses Geppetto back to health. In the end, Pinocchio is rewarded for the selflessness he ultimately cultivates. "Children who love their parents, and help them when they are sick and poor, are worthy of praise and love, even if they are not models of obedience and good behaviour."

Good versus evil is not an original theme in literature, but Collodi's approach turns Pinocchio's struggle into an all-too-human one. Who among us hasn't wanted to take the easy way out, shirk our responsibilities (even if for a short time), and get something for nothing?

There is an innocence about Pinocchio that we can forgive—his brains are made of wood after all—even when old Geppetto sells his only coat to buy the puppet a schoolbook, who in turn sells it for two pence to see the puppet show. If Collodi had chosen a real character for this part, it would be difficult indeed to find enough redeeming characteristics to make him sympathetic or interesting. But Pinocchio tries so hard, and fails so horrendously, that we cannot help but cheer him on, hoping that some day one of Collodi's lessons will stick in his head. In the process of urging Pinocchio to be the good boy, which will end all his troubles, we learn the importance of the author's messages.

In the end, virtue is its own reward, for once the puppet learns the joys of doing the right thing, he becomes in the flesh that which he has become in his heart—a real boy.

—Elizabeth Engstrom

TOR CLASSICS

☐	50424-0	ADVENTURES OF SHERLOCK HOLMES *Arthur Conan Doyle*	$2.50 Canada $3.25
☐	50422-4	ADVENTURES OF HUCK FINN *Mark Twain*	$2.50 Canada $3.25
☐	50420-8	ADVENTURES OF TOM SAWYER *Mark Twain*	$2.50 Canada $3.25
☐	50418-6	ALICE'S ADVENTURES IN WONDERLAND *Lewis Carroll*	$2.50 Canada $3.25
☐	50430-5	AROUND THE WORLD IN EIGHTY DAYS *Jules Verne*	$2.50 Canada $3.25
☐	50426-7	BILLY BUDD *Herman Melville*	$2.50 Canada $3.25
☐	50428-3	BLACK BEAUTY *Anna Sewell*	$2.50 Canada $3.25
☐	50432-1	CALL OF THE WILD *Jack London*	$2.50 Canada $3.25
☐	50438-0	CAPTAINS COURAGEOUS *Rudyard Kipling*	$2.50 Canada $3.25
☐	50434-8	A CHRISTMAS CAROL *Charles Dickens*	$2.50 Canada $3.25
☐	50436-4	A CONNECTICUT YANKEE IN KING ARTHUR'S COURT *Mark Twain*	$2.50 Canada $3.25

Buy them at your local bookstore or use this handy coupon:
Clip and mail this page with your order.

Publishers Book and Audio Mailing Service
P.O. Box 120159, Staten Island, NY 10312-0004

Please send me the book(s) I have checked above. I am enclosing $ _____
(Please add $1.50 for the first book, and $.50 for each additional book to cover postage and
handling. Send check or money order only — no CODs.)

Name _____

Address _____

City _____ State / Zip _____

Please allow six weeks for delivery. Prices subject to change without notice.

MORE TOR CLASSICS

☐	50440-2	DAISY MILLER *Henry James*	$2.50 Canada $3.25
☐	50448-8	DOCTOR JEKYLL AND MR. HYDE *Robert Louis Stevenson*	$2.50 Canada $3.25
☐	50442-9	DRACULA *Bram Stoker*	$2.50 Canada $3.25
☐	50455-0	EDGAR ALLEN POE: A Collection of Short Stories *Edgar Allen Poe*	$2.50 Canada $3.25
☐	50457-7	FRANKENSTEIN *Mary Shelley*	$2.50 Canada $3.25
☐	50459-3	THE HOUSE OF THE SEVEN GABLES *Nathaniel Hawthorne*	$2.50 Canada $3.25
☐	50467-4	THE INVISIBLE MAN *H. G. Wells*	$2.50 Canada $3.25
☐	50471-2	JOURNEY TO THE CENTER OF THE EARTH *Jules Verne*	$2.50 Canada $3.25
☐	50469-0	THE JUNGLE BOOKS *Rudyard Kipling*	$2.50 Canada $3.25
☐	50473-9	KIDNAPPED *Robert Louis Stevenson*	$2.50 Canada $3.25
☐	51956-6	THE LADY OR THE TIGER and Other Short Stories *Frank Stockton*	$2.50 Canada $3.25

Buy them at your local bookstore or use this handy coupon:
Clip and mail this page with your order.

Publishers Book and Audio Mailing Service
P.O. Box 120159, Staten Island, NY 10312-0004

Please send me the book(s) I have checked above. I am enclosing $ _____
(Please add $1.50 for the first book, and $.50 for each additional book to cover postage and
handling. Send check or money order only — no CODs.)

Name _____

Address _____

City _____ State / Zip _____

Please allow six weeks for delivery. Prices subject to change without notice.

READ TOR CLASSICS

☐	52297-4	THE LAST OF THE MOHICANS *James Fenimore Cooper*	$3.99 Canada $4.99
☐	50475-5	THE LEGEND OF SLEEPY HOLLOW *Washington Irving*	$2.50 Canada $3.25
☐	52333-4	LITTLE WOMEN *Louisa May Alcott*	$3.99 Canada $4.50
☐	52076-9	O PIONEERS! *Willa Cather*	$2.50 Canada $3.25
☐	52336-9	PRIDE AND PREJUDICE *Jane Austen*	$2.50 Canada $3.25
☐	50477-1	THE PRINCE AND THE PAUPER *Mark Twain*	$2.50 Canada $3.25
☐	50479-8	THE RED BADGE OF COURAGE *Stephen Crane*	$2.50 Canada $3.25
☐	52332-6	RIP VAN WINKLE and Other Stories *Washington Irving*	$2.50 Canada $3.25
☐	50482-8	ROBINSON CRUSOE *Daniel Defoe*	$2.50 Canada $3.25
☐	50483-6	THE SCARLET LETTER *Nathaniel Hawthorne*	$2.50 Canada $3.25
☐	50501-8	THE SECRET GARDEN *Frances Hodgson Burnett*	$3.99 Canada $4.99

Buy them at your local bookstore or use this handy coupon:
Clip and mail this page with your order.

Publishers Book and Audio Mailing Service
P.O. Box 120159, Staten Island, NY 10312-0004

Please send me the book(s) I have checked above. I am enclosing $ _____
(Please add $1.50 for the first book, and $.50 for each additional book to cover postage and
handling. Send check or money order only—no CODs.)

Name _____

Address _____

City _____ State / Zip _____

Please allow six weeks for delivery. Prices subject to change without notice.

ENJOY TOR CLASSICS

	50502-6	STORIES BY O. HENRY *O. Henry*	$2.50 Canada $3.25
☐	50502-6	STORIES BY O. HENRY *O. Henry*	$2.50 Canada $3.25
☐	50506-9	A TALE OF TWO CITIES *Charles Dickens*	$2.50 Canada $3.25
☐	50504-2	THE TIME MACHINE *H. G. Wells*	$2.50 Canada $3.25
☐	53035-7	TOM SAWYER, DETECTIVE *Mark Twain*	$2.50 Canada $3.25
☐	50508-5	TREASURE ISLAND *Robert Louis Stevenson*	$2.50 Canada $3.25
☐	50515-8	THE WAR OF THE WORLDS *H. G. Wells*	$2.50 Canada $3.25
☐	50512-3	WHITE FANG *Jack London*	$2.50 Canada $3.25
☐	50510-7	THE WIND IN THE WILLOWS *Kenneth Grahame*	$2.50 Canada $3.25
☐	50516-6	WUTHERING HEIGHTS *Emily Bronte*	$2.50 Canada $3.25